Waket

The Boy in Time

Stephen Orr was born in Adelaide in 1967, studied science and education and taught in a range of country and metropolitan schools. One of his early plays, *Attempts to Draw Jesus*, became his first novel, shortlisted for the *Australian/*Vogel's Literary Award.

Since then he has published ten novels (most recently, *Sincerely, Ethel Malley*) and a volume of short stories (*Datsunland*). He has been nominated for awards such as the Commonwealth Writers' Prize, the Miles Franklin Award and the International Dublin Literary Award.

THE
BOY IN
TIME

STEPHEN ORR

Wakefield
Press

Wakefield Press
16 Rose Street
Mile End
South Australia 5031
www.wakefieldpress.com.au

First published 2022

Cover designed by Stacey Zass
Edited by Polly Grant Butler. Wakefield Press
Typeset by Michael Deves, Wakefield Press

ISBN 978 1 74305 968 5

A catalogue record for this
book is available from the
National Library of Australia

Wakefield Press thanks
Coriole Vineyards for
continued support

Contents

Introduction

The Boy in Time

Like many, I started writing short fiction (doesn't this sound more respectable than *stories*?) well before I wrote a novella, then a novel, dripping with details and characters and plot, in the way the 'greats' (Dickens, for example, I started reading him when I was fourteen) taught us to write. These early fictions were so laboured, predictable, welded onto familiar frameworks, that a few years later, looking back over them, I decided I'd said nothing original, so, as is the ritual, took them into the backyard (a dozen or so, perhaps) and burned them. This would ensure (Kafka and Max Brod-like) there were no traces of what was most certainly rubbish (although maybe genius – how far did my capacity for self-delusion reach?). The smoke would rise as an offering to the gods of the second-rate, and they'd be appeased, leave me alone, and I could get on with something worth reading.

From a young age we learn that words are tools. If I say 'sunrise', that's enough (though some writers insist on making it painfully clear). Sex, more than enough. The term 'drunkard' is useful, but just as limiting. This is the art, the balance, between what's kept in and excised. We needn't hear why her uncle wore taffeta, but it's interesting, and took three days of research, so why not? We know there are millions of fictions written every year, thousands published; there are MFAs and creative writing degrees and people get up at four am to describe their version of the universe, or ignore their starving children to turn out another neglected poem. We insist upon the perfect metaphor, feel we've conquered the world when we cut another adjective, the twist, ah! you didn't see it coming, did you, *this* is why she was murdered, *here* are the reasons for the divorce, all of this, as words, again, fail to counteract our own little man-made Coriolis effect. Somehow, we believe, we'll get what others have missed. The nifty shift in tense, the unique stream-of-consciousness, the Sebaldian photos of desiccated fish.

I'm most interested in writers who can teach me something. Maybe this started at Sunday school, where some young teacher (determined to save our suburban souls) asked, 'Who's heard of the parable of the mustard seed?' Of course, we'd only heard the parable of Steve Austin, Six Million Dollar Man, or the demigod H.R. Pufnstuf, so this was an intriguing question. As she read: 'The kingdom of heaven is like a mustard seed a man plants in his field.' Going on to explain how this seed grows into 'the largest of garden plants, and becomes a tree'. Me, my sister, the others thinking (perhaps): Why are we hearing about ... oh, hold on, it's not actually *about* the mustard seed! The clues were there: the teacher's authentic smile, the simile-peppered text, the reluctance of the Author to give anything away, the insistence that the reader or listener makes his or her own meaning.

From there, the journey continued. With *The Pickwick Papers* and *Oliver Twist* came Dickens's short fiction; with *Tortilla Flat* and *Of Mice and Men*, 'The Chrysanthemums'. Patrick White revealed himself in new ways with his more theatrical, mystical and arcane stories (the ones he didn't think would make it to novelhood?) with *The Cockatoos* and *The Burnt Ones*. There was, it seemed, a connection between the small and big; the simple ideas and fleshed out epics. Either way, one seemed necessary for the other, although with Jorge Luis Borges I learnt that short fiction wasn't the poor cousin of novels, but the germinal seed, Whitman's procreant urge, the things closest to what our ancestors grunted over Neolithic campfires. Clay statuettes made in the images of gods; base metals heated over ancient fires to make mythical alloys that would, as the centuries passed, become tools for the assembly of Great Literature. Sung by nineteenth century mastersingers in Nuremberg; Portnoy rhapsodising behind locked doors; Leopold Bloom contemplating the snotgreen, scrotum-tightening sea.

Borges made it clear. Picking up in 1928 from where God had left off. Baltasar Espinosa staying at the Los Alamos ranch 'south of the small town of Junin' with his cousin Daniel. When Daniel is called away to Buenos Aires, Espinosa allows the Gutre family ('they had come from Inverness and had arrived in the New World – undoubtedly as peasant labourers – in the early nineteenth century') to move into a room beside his. He finds an English language Bible and starts reading them the Gospel of Mark (and the story finds its title, and framework). The family members take it too literally and, when Espinosa sleeps with their young daughter, use Mark's lessons for their own ends: '… they cursed him, spat on him, and drove him back to the house … Espinosa realised what awaited him on the other side of the door … they had torn down the roof beams to build a cross.' Nothing to see here. A simple moral, but no moral. Still, the largest of garden plants had become a tree. Nothing didactic or moralistic, no lessons to be taught or learnt by seven-year-olds with their socks pulled up to their knees. Upon discovering Borges, and other masters of short fiction, the way forward was clear – say less, say it with less certainty, remove everything you can, make the idea so compelling it can never be unread, forgotten, discounted. Vonnegut created rules, and writers love rules, don't they? Be a sadist. Start as close to the end as possible. Give the reader as much information as possible as soon as possible. But for me it was always the *idea*. Everything else was, and is, confetti.

Short stories can be anything we want them to be. The gem of the novel you know you'll never write (I've saved myself years of work through condensing ideas into fictions for *The Saturday Paper*); a description of the way the man at the creamery scoops the ice cream, stops, wipes his brow, gazes out the window, continues; pleas for change; moments of horror (Flannery O'Connor's adventures into gothic Catholicism); apprentice pieces; testing the water for something larger (Malcolm Lowry's short version of *Under the Volcano*). The best examples of short fiction can't be canned, labelled, opened and consumed at will. No writing course can teach them, no formula derived, no deeper understanding of some perfect model that leads to others (although this is how we mistakenly keep teaching fiction). Maybe that's why there was only one Bible, and even that was a heavily edited and curated collection of fictions.

Stories like Juan Rulfo's 'Do You Hear the Dogs Barking?' Here, we encounter a father carrying his injured son, Ignacio, across his shoulders as they cross mountains in search of the town of Tonaya. Why? What's there? What answers? What redemptions? What's happened to Ignacio? The boy tells his father, 'Put me down here – leave me here – you go on alone.' But the old man is determined, and disgruntled. 'I'm not doing all this for you. I'm doing it for your dead mother. Because you were her son … she's the one who gives me courage, not you. From the first you've caused me nothing but trouble, humiliation and shame.' As we long for some explanation, but realise it's not, it never will be, forthcoming.

Introduction

In 2017, after publishing short fiction for a dozen years, I selected the best published and unpublished works and released them in a collection titled *Datsunland*. What I left out, I see in retrospect, were my attempts at being funny, making a point, trying to convince readers of this or that – the lessons writers have to keep learning over and over. There were one or two that I wouldn't, shouldn't, have included. Luckily, collections allow a few moments of grace for the lesser to be subsumed by the greater. Mercy! But the truly great collections make no concessions. J.D. Salinger's *Nine Stories*. 'A Perfect Day for Bananafish' strikes a perfect balance between the ordinary and tragic, as Seymour Glass unwinds before us, as the god Salinger (with a little help from William Maxwell) plays with his characters, describes their moles, their reading ('Sex is Fun – or Hell') and what happens when fish get banana fever ('it's a terrible disease'). Or perhaps Chekov's 'The Lady with the Dog', Katherine Mansfield's 'The Garden Party', O'Connor's 'You Can't Be Any Poorer Than Dead'), the first remarkable reading of Kafka's 'Metamorphosis', or the way one keeps returning to Joyce's 'The Dead', feeling, somehow, there's something you missed last time.

Here, then, is my second collection. I've tried to include a selection, a cross section of styles from experimental ('The boy in time') to problematic ('Incident near Hoxtolgay Town'), tragic ('Mrs Meiners has gone to get chalk') to the stories that just appeared, ready-made ('Violettowne'). I found some ideas in newspapers, magazines, books. For example, 'The leaf winds', the last days of World War II, the actions of a family faced with uncomfortable truths. Something overheard ('Violettowne'); a metaphor taken to its logical conclusion ('The death of Tomas Kirja'); and sometimes, a realignment of the real world with my own. There are ghosts, sex, death and murder; the way in which (according to Borges) heaven and hell seem out of proportion; and children, cast into the horrors of the world we, and our old people, have made for them. The boy in time running for his life, wandering the desert, trying to make himself understood, survive. These stories have washed up on the beach over many years; only some were found and collected, others given to charity or, again, offered up to the flame. Maybe that's the fate of every story we tell? They were published in *The Saturday Paper, Burning House Press, Island, Westerly, Meanjin, The Saltbush Review* and the anthology *Thrill Me*. As I've tired of the predictable, I've experimented. Will continue to do so, until I'm either unfathomable, surplus to need, or worst of all, boring. Then I'll settle into my memories, and the visions that elude words.

The leaf winds

Peter Maier wanders the shaded lawns beneath the birches and elms; small steps, where the leaves (in the boundary between yard and forest) surrender to the late autumn winds. Snowing russet and rouge in some pattern, some plan, some schedule that means not too many, not too few fall at a time. He follows the path around the kitchen garden and remembers the times he's helped his father turn the soil, plant the carrots, the potatoes. Like this, wandering, unsure where to stand, where to go, what to think about what his mother calls the ending. He can hear the artillery a few kilometres away. They've been warned – later today, or tomorrow.

Peter Maier wears his best Sunday clothes. His mother laid them out for him and his father watched as he got dressed, saying, 'It needn't be such a drama.' But, by definition, it does, and will be, and this is why he's so anxious.

His father comes to the back door and calls, 'Peter, your aunt's here.'

'So?'

'It's time to come in now.'

His father – who up until recently was mayor of their small town, sixty-three kilometres from the capital – is also dressed in his best suit: dark, with pinstripes, shoes (polished that morning), a new shirt and favourite tie. 'Peter?'

'No.'

'Now!'

Peter just stares at him. He knows the procedure. He knows why they're dressed in their best and why his father's brother has arrived and his mother's sister, and why his own sister has sat, staring out of the window all morning. He sits on a low bough of a linden and notices his pocket-knife, left open, from where he's been peeling peaches. He closes the knife and places it in his pocket and his father calls again, and he refuses again. He feels a strange sensation in his chest, and down below. Perhaps this is God (he's been told) preparing him for what comes next. Although he doesn't believe in all that (his mother for, his father against). And anyway, what's it matter now? It's past the point of reasoning, of talking, the family meetings, the discussions about who's done what to whom, his father the mayor, the camp, on the edge of town.

Peter loosens his tie. He takes a deep breath, feels the sun on his face, notices the high clouds and wants to go inside to get his book. But then a strange plane flies over and they look up and his father says, 'They'll be landing soon.' His fat arms, and solid body; his walrus moustache, trimmed the previous evening (by his mother). The party badge on his lapel. 'What, you'd have them arrest me?'

Peter waits.

'And you. You know what would happen then?'

'Not if I'm twelve, and Anni, seven, what could they …?'

'I told you.'

I just want to stay here, Peter thinks. I want to eat oranges and read about Brazil and how toucans got their colours. 'You, then,' he says.

'Together. It's time.'

'No.'

'I don't want to have to get angry.'

Peter can see his father's face turning red, the steam (he'd laugh with Anni) venting from his ears, his eyes popping from his skull (as they rolled on the grass, just here, imitating the way his spoke). *'Don't make me ask you again.'*

'Peter!'

'No!'

Peter Maier runs from his yard, along the side of the house, jumping across the front garden, until he's on Forstweg. He takes a moment to think, where should I go? As the artillery continues, and what sounds like panzerfaust and rifles, the tack of machine pistol in the cold morning.

'Peter?'

His father, following him to the street, saying, 'What's the point of this? Now you need to be with your family.'

Peter sees his sister in the front window, her eyes pleading with him to run, he thinks. She mouths something, but he can't tell what, then she shouts something, then his uncle closes the curtain.

'You'd rather they strung you up somewhere?'

'They won't.'

'I showed you the pictures.'

He had. Whole families – parents, boys, still in uniform, with their hair parted, their faces washed, their necks at strange angles.

Peter decides. He turns and runs along the street, and his dad calls after him. He sprints, past his friend's Willi's house, three bikes lying on the gravel drive, past the Wilhelm sisters' pruned roses, shrubs filling the morning with lavender and spiced-apple.

'Peter!'

His father runs as best he can, more a sort of waddle, stopping and starting, leaning on fence posts.

An army truck goes past and five or six soldiers call something to him, then laugh, then one indicates he should return to his father. This is how it's been, these last years. Everyone telling him what, where, how, sing this or that – like there was a plan he, and the rest of his troop, couldn't fathom. That had led him here.

Peter Maier continues past his school, the lawns still neat, the flags still flying. They'll have to be taken down. They'll convince the Russians they were enjoying it. Anyway, the Reds will see it all at the camp. He's walked past it a hundred times with his sister, the men in grey tunics, the dogs forever barking, the chimneys forever smoking, the station called Z, because it was the last place (everyone knew) you ever visited.

He thinks of going into the school, but guesses they'll check there, too. So he continues, towards Str. den Einheit. The shoe shop, boarded up; the grocer, its doors always open; the paper shop where Mr Goldblatt once worked (telling him about Ali Baba and Robinson Crusoe); the town hall where he'd visit his father after school. The big, oak-panelled office, his secretary, her typewriter (on which he'd practise his name).

An old man stops him and says, 'Where are you going, son? They'll be here in an hour. Where's your father?'

Peter points down the road and his father waddles towards him, calling, 'Hold him, Stefan.'

So the old man holds him by the arm, and he struggles to get away, but Stefan won't let go. Soon, his father catches up, takes a moment to get his breath and then goes to slap him across the face, but remembers the day, the time, the plans.

'I'm too old for this.'

What does that matter? Peter thinks.

'Where will you go?' his father asks Stefan.

He points to the far end of the street and a barricade, hastily set up. A few men and boys, still in their uniforms, and Peter says, 'I'll go there, I'll help them. We should fight, shouldn't we, instead of …?'

'They won't last five minutes,' his father says. 'I told you, Peter, I can't afford to get caught.'

The old man lets go and Peter glares at his father. He looks in the window of Dorfmann's and notices new shoes, reduced. This means there's still hope. Life can, and will, continue with new shoes.

But the guns pound and the glass rattles and his father says, 'Are you coming home?'

Peter feels his legs, cold, and the need to pee, but dares not.

His father opens his pill case and reminds him of what he calls 'our one consolation'. He says, 'Just like falling asleep.'

But Peter overheard them the previous night. How the prussic acid stops the lungs absorbing air, and there are moments, a minute maybe, where you can't breathe, and shake and piss yourself. Before you die.

The three of them stand, listening, thinking, then the old man asks if his father has a spare pill, and takes one, and continues down the road.

Peter can't see a way forward. His hands are small, he is good at piano. He can carve eagles from soft pine (his sister has a shelf full). He can do long division better than anyone in his class. For what? The pills are small for what they can do. They are white, like egg shells. They look like mints in his father's palm.

After the Fall

It wasn't true that Ferdinand IV was the son of Ferdinand III and he, in turn, was the son of Ferdinand II, and so forth. For a start, Matthias II (26 June 1608 – 20 March 1640) came in between, and he was the most popular king of all. Lots of old men with chin whiskers and military uniforms covered in badges and medals they hadn't earned. But what's that matter now? The statue is six foot eight, whereas Matthias was barely five foot (the king asked the sculptor, another few inches, and since he was working in the shadow of the guillotine, he obliged). It's made from marble and weighs two hundred kilograms. Matthias's left hand is missing. No one knows why, but it's missing. He's dressed in a marble frock coat, marble boots, breeches, full dress uniform. He was nearing thirty when he sat for the sculptor and, although he had no idea, would only live another two years.

It wasn't true, either, that Matthias was a despot. All of these rumours, all of this *revisionism* came later. It is true that he had several African colonies, and each of these supplied raw materials – coal, oil, iron, slaves – for the Motherland, but he wasn't a despot, he didn't suspend parliament, close a single newspaper, have anyone beheaded for anything he or she didn't do (as far as we know). And he was enlightened. He founded two universities (one named after Rousseau, a personal hero), the state theatre, the state opera, Europe's seventh biggest zoological gardens (he was a man of science), a gallery full of the great artists of the day, on and on, like this. A remarkable man.

Although he had his enemies. Before his early death there'd been several attempts on his life. Possibly because of misaligned power structures, family issues, things like this, but also, maybe, perhaps (and this has never been investigated) because of his dealings in tobacco, thousands of acres of illegally felled forests, an early (but unverified) massacre of West African natives. You decide. That's the funny thing about history. Everyone has an opinion. But, of course, everyone wasn't there. In fact, after long enough, no one was there. So what's or who's to say what's right or wrong or moral, immoral? Who's to say whether such and such acted properly, cared for his or her people, showed compassion? I mean, countries don't run on fresh air (not that I want to seem an apologist, this early in my story), they need money, and plenty of it, to pay for armies to invade more countries to secure more rubber, oil, timber, to build more homes and power more heaters and … like this, as history shows. So let's make it clear, none of us – me, you, the so-called academics – have any right to judge poor Matthias, one-handed Matthias (someone claimed it was overuse – 'Matthias the Masturbator' – though that, too, was never verified).

So, a statue of the king lying on the ground, and the man's attached a rope under the arms, between the legs – joined them, harnessed them to a leather bridle arrangement he straps across his shoulders and chest most days (he has Saturday off) – and pulls Matthias along the road, along the street, along the path, through the park, Highway Number One, the A121, back roads, country lanes, he pulls Matthias, all day every day, stopping at around six at night, pitching his tent, lighting his fire, cooking an egg and bacon or rabbit or something he's trapped. Like this. Every day except Saturday. Then he lays out his swag, reads for an hour, studies the stars, falls asleep, gets up at five, sets off, dragging Matthias through a paddock here, along a laneway there, a dry river bed, back to the asphalt. But he has to keep going, because history asks, no, *demands* he drags the statue of Matthias II across the nation he once colonised (with hardly a shot fired, hardly any loss of life – although then again, there was the cholera).

As I mentioned, he's no longer a young man. He's been dragging Matthias for thirteen years, and (he figures) he's covered one tenth of the monarch's former colony. He knows he has to keep going, keep trapping rabbits, drinking water from puddles. He knows he has to visit another dozen cities, fifty towns, hundreds of small villages that, in their time, raised their own statues of the monarch. A long way to go, and he's tired and lonely and sometimes at night he thinks of the woman who was his wife and tries to remember her name (Susan, or Sally, something), tries to recall his children's names, although with the progress of time, he's forgetting, it's leaving him, in fact, now he's not even sure he had children. Maybe they were his neighbour's children? Maybe he's getting confused? Yes, confused. This, he suspects, is from the strain. Maybe it's dementia, maybe Alzheimer's, his father lost his marbles when he was sixty. His father, or a neighbour, a friend, a work colleague? Because he used to work. He used to have a job. He's not sure what he did, but he thinks (when he's lying there at night, or during the day, dragging Matthias along a deserted highway) he might have done something with tyres, which makes sense, because they would have been made from rubber, and that's where all the problems began. Maybe he fit tyres to cars? Maybe the thousands of cars that pass him every day have tyres that *he* once fit? Because there are so many cars and trucks and buses and carts, all of this. Traversing the country. Some just drive past, some toot him for being on the road, some slow and someone calls (something like), 'Where are you off to today?' And he tells them. Some stop and offer him a drink, and sometimes meat and vegetables and fruit, and that night he eats well (as he studies the position of the Big Dog). One time, someone came too close, clipped Matthias (though he later glued his head back on), sent both of them flying into a drainage ditch beside the road, and he stopped himself with his hands and broke a wrist, but a doctor in the next town set it, for free, and it really didn't bother him, it didn't get in the way, it didn't matter, it didn't slow his journey. So, in short, it's hard. Because of

(a) the weight of the monarch
(b) the nature of the road surfaces
(c) his sore shoulders and chest and back and legs
(d) weather (hot days, cold days, rain, dust storms, lightning, thunder)
(e) wild animals (he carries a rifle to ward off the big cats)
(f) the isolation
(g) the mental stress (lately, he feels, he's becoming more depressed, more uncertain about the nature of his journey)
(h) thoughts of what else he might be doing
(i) other things, some too personal to mention

Gravel is easiest. The statue glides across the gravel. Sand is worst. Matthias sinks, and sometimes he, the man, has to dig him out. This can take hours, and then he's late for the next town, but then again, what does it matter? There was a time he'd be given a welcome in a new village, or city, the mayor, councillors, the local brass band perhaps, a few hundred citizens. But that doesn't happen anymore. Maybe, he thinks (as he walks) people have become more apathetic, lazy, less interested in their history, less willing to think through the issues? Or maybe everyone is busier these days? Or maybe, maybe Matthias doesn't mean to them what he means to him. Perhaps people have changed their minds about the monarch's achievements. For example, one day, perhaps a month ago, he arrived in a small village at four in the afternoon, sat in front of the post office, two women came along, studied the statue, summoned two men who were (he assumed) their boyfriends, and before long one of these men was pissing on the ex-king. He, the man, rushed over, pushed him aside, demanded to know what he was doing, and he said, 'What, are you some sort of nut?'

'Hardly. If I don't do this, who will?'

And the young man (zipping up): 'How do you think people feel, seeing such a thing ... you stupid old fool. How do you think? You certainly won't be raising your statue here.'

All of this aside, the journey must continue. To be fair, and despite all of the complaining (mine and his), the man enjoys his odyssey. He enjoys the mornings, when he watches hawks thermalling above a field, diving for field mice. The fresh, honey-smack smell of wet crops after rain. His tannin-stained country stretching out to the horizon, stopping, waiting in a haze, sucking (or being sucked) into the sky. He loves marvelling at the airliners and their contrails and the thought of who's in them, where they're going, who they'll meet on their own journey. He loves the cold fronts breaking the hot days, and he loves being alone as much as he hates it. He loves not having to listen to people on television selling dog food, or promising to build a football stadium if they're elected, and he loves not having to drive a car, being caught in traffic, tailgated, paying insurance, mowing his lawn and fixing his roof, all of the little things he used to like, love, put up with, he can't remember, he can't be sure. He loves not having to listen to the man next door, his angle grinder, his barking rottweiler, and when he once said something, this man replied, 'It's a free country, isn't it? Or is there some law you haven't told me about?' Matthias was a great lawmaker, too. He taxed the rich, ensured the poor had unemployment benefits, stopped people defaming each other in newspapers, lots and lots of things, but that, the man thinks, is what people have forgotten.

He also loves music, and sings to himself as he walks. Mozart, Beethoven, Duke Ellington, lots of things. His mother (and he thinks of her now, and becomes sad, but says to himself, stop it!) gave him piano lessons, and as he walks he plays the pieces he learnt in his head, or better still, recites the poems his father taught him. Often, he thinks, he realises, he wouldn't be anywhere else. Maybe, he fancies, his journey has nothing to do with the monarch? This seems strange, because he knows it does, he knows the purpose of his journey is to spread the word. And it started like this. He was standing in the park beside his house, and there was Matthias II, his missing hand, pink paint all over his head and body, a cardboard sign: 'NO PRIDE IN GENOCIDE'. He watched as a group of maybe ten, twelve young men arrived with tools (hammers, crow bars), started working on the base, loosened the king, attached a rope, gathered on the lawn and pulled slowly, bit by bit – as Matthias wobbled, leaned, fell on the path, and there was celebration, applause, singing. And he thought, Do they know what they're doing? But this was neither the time nor place to speak up. Chances were they'd attack him, verbally perhaps, but even physically, they looked angry, ready for a fight. So he just stood and waited and the next day, drafted a letter to the newspaper, but he never sent it, because he knew if he did someone at his tyre dealership (he assumes) would disagree and he'd be in a heap of trouble, so better to leave it to those who knew better – historians, politicians, writers. And he did. And he waited, and waited, got so angry (after a few months) that he decided. One morning. Arrived in the park, harnessed himself to history, started dragging the old boy south, towards the bad lands, the lands of those eternally forgotten, put out with the dog, buried, hosed off the driveway, put in a box in the shed, thrown in the skip, all of this.

All of which is how he got here, now, on the road to some town with accents above its vowels. There's been a storm, but it's passed, but it's still windy and this, perhaps, is the best walking weather, because it cools him, his hair in his eyes, all of it. It cools him. He thinks. He thinks this. If everything I've ever done has come to this ... then what was the purpose? Of being born. And thinks of the day he watched a duck and her ten ducklings in his pool, and one couldn't get out, so she took the other nine and left, and didn't come back, and he watched the lone duckling swimming back and forth, up and down, left and right, across the pool, until she ran out of puff, just floated, and he scooped her from the pool and left her in the reeds and the next day she was gone and he wondered, wonders, still, all the time, what became of her? Did a snake happen by? Did she find her mother and siblings? Or did she just disappear, into the arms of some duck god? That'd be good. That'd be to hope for, but it was unlikely, he thought now. Life is never so neat, so simple, so fair. That's it. Fair. Life wasn't designed to be fair, it was designed to give the other nine a chance, and if he's worried about the lone duckling, then that's his fault, and probably explains why he's in such a perilous situation now.

Either way, this day, I have to get to this day, this story is taking me too long to tell and some editor, somewhere, will be itching to cut it, this bit, perhaps, so the reader will have more time to watch television, choose the best type of dog food. So the man is walking along in the post-storm morning when a child emerges from the gorse, the bushes, who knows, and says, 'Where are you going?' The man says, 'Where did you come from?' The boy says the city, and points east, although the man's not sure which city, and asks, and the boy says it doesn't matter, does it, what's that thing you're dragging? The man says Matthias II. He was left in a park. The boy asks why. The man says history had finished with him, as it will finish with all of us, you, me, and ten minutes after we're gone, who'll care, who'll remember us, son … what's your name? But the boy says, 'They won't forget me.' The man asks why, why will you be so memorable? But again, the boy just shrugs.

Strangely, the boy decides to accompany the man (for a way, at least) on his journey. The boy is all white, cricket clothes, a red stain on his thigh, he's dragging a bag full of (the man supposes) bats, balls, water, things like this. As they walk, the man says, 'Are you expected somewhere?' The boy says no, the game's finished, we lost again, I was out for a duck, but I don't care because I don't like cricket anyway. The man asks why, and the boy explains, his father was a great cricketer, represented the country, went to England, Australia, the West Indies, all of the usual places, and now he's retired he lives his life *vicariously* (the man's impressed with the boy's vocabulary) through him. 'For example, every afternoon we spend three hours in the nets … and I practise my bowling, my batting, and he gives me tips, but they're always the same tips he's given me before, but I don't say anything because I know it means a lot to him.' The man thinks this isn't so bad, tells him, the boy sees the man's struggling, offers to help, the man says no, you have your bag, and the boy says so what, I can come back for it, hides it in some bushes, puts the rope around his chest, and they set off. Soon, the boy says, 'This is so heavy, how do you manage?' The man tells him he just does, he's used to it, when you believe in what you're doing it doesn't bother you.

Like this. They continue like this. The man tells the boy his father was nothing like (he assumes) the boy's father. 'He was always reading, writing essays no one would publish. Things like the loss of civic values ... I suppose he was living in the past, but maybe all of us live in the past, do you think?' Again, the boy just shrugs. The man tells him his father wrote novels, too, and a few were published, but no one bought them, and he still has boxes of unsold books in the shed, and would you, son, like a few, but the boy just shrugs. The man says his father also wrote poetry. He loved poetry best, and would you like to hear one of his poems? The boy doesn't, but guesses to say no would seem rude, so he says fine, let me hear one, and the man begins:

It was surprising that Carl should straighten the pictures on
the mantel
The one of young Fred up a tree, sketching, bitten lip and
crossed ankles
Aged seven, legs hanging out of the carriage
Like there was no chance, no chance at all he could fall.

The man says this one is called 'Surprising' and it's about an old couple whose son has died, and they drive off a cliff. You see, my father was talented, but no one cared, no one cares anything anymore for things that matter. The boy asks what, what matters, and the man stops and indicates Matthias and says, 'The king, for example. A cultured man. But no one remembers that now.' The boy asks if this is why the man is dragging him around the country, and the man says yes, I suppose it is. I suppose we all have an axe to grind. The boy asks what axe, but the man continues:

> *Strange how Carl said yes, and indicated the chromium sky and said what a day for it*
> *And felt nothing of the loss of remainderless subtractions, moments of grace in the back yard, eleven pm, a glimpse of Venus, and Fred saying (from his room), What you looking at, Dad?*
> *Surprising, that even now, and after the Fall, he'd ask*
> *And surprising that life could make itself so clear, so known, so understood, so perfect and not too hot, not too cold, not too windy, not too bright*
> *And asked for nothing in return for what it had given, and taken away.*

They stop again, and the boy asks, 'What had life given the old couple?' The man thinks about this for a moment, and replies, 'Can't you see? All of this.' Indicating the green fields in flower. Then the boy says, 'So what did it take away?' The man shrugs, and says he's not sure, you'd have to ask my father, but he's long dead, so maybe we'll never know, and maybe we'll just have to work it out for ourselves. But the boy's not happy with this. They've walked several miles, it's getting late, his shoulders and back are sore, and now he'll get in trouble for arriving home so late, so he wants to know what, what did it take away? But again, the man just shrugs, and the boy gets angry, and he says, 'We might as well raise it here then? If it doesn't matter?' The man says no, he has hundreds of places to go yet, and the boy says they don't care, no one cares, so maybe this'll do, maybe this spot, beside the rest stop, will do? After a moment, the man sighs, empties every bit of air from his lungs. He looks at the sun, low in the sky, smells the damp wheat, and something dead in the grass, and says, 'You're right. As good as anywhere. Give me a hand, will you?'

The quickest way home

Patrick Hagan sits watching an old woman, someone's gran or nan, loading a boy into a car. BMW i3, as per his salary package, long gone. He studies her dents and guesses she can't drive, but what's that matter, she has a BMW and he has a Mazda. The way she scolds the six- or seven-year-old, stands with her hands on her hips, shakes her head and says something he can't hear. He decides he dislikes her, immensely. But there are plenty like her: mums with pigeon pairs in their blazers, socks down around their ankles, carrying trombones and violins, as a hi-vis teacher waves to the kids and it's all so *happy*. He finds his smokes, searches the pack, but it's empty. The Ziploc bag with the roach, but again, empty. The few cans on the floor, and he reaches over, picks one up, drains the last bit of sun-warmed scotch, continues watching the boys coming through the gates.

There he is! He gets out, calls: 'Harry, over here a minute.' The boy stops, looks at him strangely, but decides to do as he's told. Drags his cricket bag over to Patrick, ex-accountant, ex-partner, ex-worker, -person, anything. But Patrick doesn't care, because it's past that now, it's decided, and what'll be will be. As Harry (he's sure that's his name) approaches he squints and angles his head and says, 'Hi.' Patrick's sure. He remembers the photo from his boss's desk, and from when Rod showed him his family snaps, when was it, a Christmas dinner, last year, the year before, before he was called into his office. Yes, he's sure this is the boy. And he says, 'Your dad asked if I could pick you up.' Again, the boy's confused, concerned (he's smart, Rod's told him he's smart). Patrick tells him Rod was busy and asked if he could pick him up and take him home. The boy still isn't sure, but Patrick knows he has no time to lose, because what if the boy's mother, Cyn, Sally, some fucked-up name, arrives trying to pick him up, and it all comes out?

Patrick (busy checking for CCTV) says, 'And your mum can't come, so I'll have to do, okay?' Even now, he's studying the boy's semi-familiar face, his high cheekbones, sweptback hair, trying to convince himself this *is* the best course of action. For what's transpired. Rod closing the door and telling him it's worse than he thought, he can't keep paying seventeen staff. Continuing. Unfolding. But still, standing outside St Thomas's, full of personal rage, this small, nagging doubt grows and Patrick wonders *if* ... Either way, it doesn't matter, because he's come too far, he's committed, and Harry's seen him and how the hell would he explain this now? Then Harry says, 'But I thought ...?' Patrick wonders if he knows, if he's been told, if he's heard something around the dinner table? He says to the boy, 'You thought what ...?' But Harry just shrugs, decides, loads his bags in the back seat and gets in the car. He removes the smokes, the TAB slips, the McDonald's wrappers from under his arse, and says, 'I thought Dad said you'd quit?' No, no, no, Patrick says, and he starts the car, checks no one's watching, pulls out and heads down the oak-lined avenue. And now it's done, he thinks. He hears Rod explaining how someone has to go ... and this is about the hardest thing I've ever done, Patrick. Well, not the hardest, Patrick thinks, studying the boy's badges, his piping, his Windsor-knotted tie, his small, bony hands, perfect teeth and long, scotch-coloured legs.

Patrick turns onto Payneham Road, wipes the syrupy grog from his lips and says, 'Big day?' Right onto Osmond Terrace, and he asks Harry, he says, 'I bet you were surprised to see me?' Yes, the boy says, because he can only remember having seen Patrick once or twice, a staff event, and when he and his girlfriend, who was it, Terese, maybe, dropped by for drinks. The boy says, 'You're the one who writes novels, aren't you?' Patrick doesn't reply. He did, he wrote one, it won an award but no one would publish it, but he thinks now, this might make a good novel, about what happens when you fuck your employees around, when you give them two weeks' notice when you know they've got a million dollar mortgage. The boy says, 'I was thinking of becoming a writer,' and Patrick laughs, almost runs into a van, says, 'That'd be the dumbest decision of your life.' But he doesn't want to give too much away. That'd make it difficult. Although this seemed like a good idea half an hour ago, not so much now. The kid's got a fresh face, and a quiet, unassuming voice, he twists his legs together and says things like, 'That school's got so many dodgy teachers,' and he, Patrick, feels the need, the desire, to start a conversation, but knows he can't. That would ruin everything, Rod telling him he'll find a new job soon, and there's Terese, eh, she can help you out for a while? The boy says, 'Dad wants me to work for him, but I couldn't think of anything worse. An accountant. *Fuck*.'

Patrick can't help but smile. The kid says *fuck*, and now he's smelling the Ziploc bag and asking where he gets his roach. A red light, but Patrick guesses he might as well run it, then the sun blinds him, and the world seems different to what it was. It seems like there's some story, some narrative from which he's strayed, mainly because of his impatience. The gear in the boot, sitting, waiting, so there's no chance of it coming back to him. The route he's planned. Harry saying this isn't the quickest way home, and him trying to decide whether it is, or not.

The muddy sunshine

Maybe I can calculate my way out of it? Terminal velocity, 54 m/s, @ 37,000 feet, which gives me about two and half minutes (not exactly, but considering, that'll do). To do what? Think of a way out? Go over every detail and see if I could've done it better? Reassess my life via Nairobi, South B Hospital, seven and a half pounds, small bassinet in the corner of a mud-brick home, loving mother and father, primary school, high school, and Mrs Otieno telling Mama the boy's some sort of mathematical genius. Straight to my senior year, university, and here I am, falling, third year B. Comp. Sc. branded Nike and American Dreams, Kamau in my head saying a discrete time system in which the output is equal to the input: y [n] = x [n-1], and Shana, my girlfriend telling me if I get to London, if I *get to London*, but Kamau rabbiting on a sine x over x type function and its Fourier transform complement. All of this, and here's me doing the maths, a minute and fifty seconds, forty, thirty, and I can see the suburbs of London, far below the Dreamliner's wheel-well, the big tyres coming down, grabbing for a hand-hold, but falling towards some strange infinity in the shape of suburbs (becoming clearer), streets, homes, and a fat man in underpants sunning himself in his yard, the seconds ticking down, but luckily, time waiting for me to catch up. Shana, Shana, Shana, shouldn't have listened to the stuff about Big Ben (there, in the distance) and how someone as smart as me could make millions, lecture at a university, a proper one, not a rubbishy Nairobi one, and I could tell people, like Kamau, suppose my function is the cube root of seven minus 9: $f(x) = \sqrt[3]{7} - 9$

Fifty-four metres per second? No asking time to slow, to reconsider how I got up this morning, slipped on my American shoes, my American pants, read a magazine full of American dreams, before Shana came in and made sure I had everything ready, three coats, four pairs of pants, and the bottle of oxygen I'd bought for $50. See, I'm not stupid (remember that about me in fifty-nine seconds' time). I did the research. Found that most people fall out on take-off (online schematic: 'Boeing XC45 2003'), worked out how to get in, where to sit, where to hold. Shana's brother, a luggage handler, counting his $100. People became unconscious, and when the wheels dropped, fell to their death. Most were never found because they ended up in the ocean. A strange, quiet, anonymous, singularly terrifying but publicly invisible death of the black man, the cheap life, the numbers hardly worth counting. And it wasn't a good survival rate. But I'd calculated it, over and over, to make sure, understand the curl of F dot n in respect to the faces, dozens of them going through my head, imagining how it would end, the sunbather getting bigger, looking up, noticing something small and black falling from the sky. What sort of equation could solve such a ridiculous problem except the knowledge that a third component of zero $F(x, y) = $ <p, q> = <F1, F2, 0> sometimes helps. Sometimes doesn't, still falling, and he's squinting now, unsure, but thinking maybe it's a black angel, or dog, lost from BA Cargo.

If I ask nicely, can you slow, can you stop, time? 54m/s per second is terminally fast, barely a moment to remember my mother's face, her voice, the way she'd hold me at the school gate and say no, no, never, I'll never let you go, you're warm and wonderful and beautiful, my son. Do you know how much

I love you? So much I prayed to God to give you a gift and he did! The smell of her powder, her arms, her breath, and Papa's sweat, the feel of his hand on my chest, slowing my breathing when it got too fast. Mama! Papa! The man in his underpants standing, calling for someone, and a woman running out. I could almost wave to them, but none of it should've happened like this. The rewarming, the reoxygenation, who else would've known? The hypothermia, the big wheels squeezing the intestines out of your arse, the going mad (yes, I read, it can happen that quickly), the decompression, the nitrogen embolism, all of it calculated neatly, nicely, on the back of a legal pad, completing the transform $x(n) = a\psi \, u[n] \; 0<a<1$.

I can almost call down to him, tell him to be careful, make room. Although maybe it's more a question of physics. Newton explaining how it would end with an apple, force, mass, acceleration, although I can't vary any of these coefficients. Just ask time to slow, to stop, so I can come to rest an inch above the earth, like Wile E. Coyote, every night on the Astor 23X in the window of the Tabaka radio shop. Nope. Mama telling me to work through each of the problems slowly, sitting beside me for hours, taking me to the exams, me scribbling $x(n) = u[n] \; 0<a<1$ as a way of making sense of the world, although there were always the dead dogs, the rapists, and Shana telling me we could do better, Max. We could live in a Manhattan penthouse. If you climbed out of the wheel well, claimed asylum.

54 m/s. It's not slowing. His wife's shaking her head. Mama smelling much the same, but with the clematis coming in the window. Quick, quick, quick, it *can* be solved, Max! Full marks, son. The world's your oyster (opening beneath you) if you're good at maths. Coming up to meet you, the fields of green, the trees, the high street with more people noticing, pointing

up, and me at age six, running with the boys along Lusaka
Road, kicking the patched ball (Papa's), making a goal from a
cardboard box, my small legs, our small legs, running about in
the muddy sunshine, the way we cheated, laughed, jumped on
top of each other, fell to the earth, grazed knees and broke teeth,
so long, not really, six, seven years ago, and always the dream
of better shoes and pants if you could become American (via
London). Newton making it clear that for every action there's a
(what was it? the drift towards infinity, the value of x, y, no, e, e
= 2.718281828459 … going on and on forever, never resolving,
because nothing irrational ever did, and in the end, ever could).

Sitting, on the day of my entrance examination, trying to work
out how $1/N$ transform x $(y) = -N(t)$ could answer one of several
questions about underpants, all white and baggy, the powder to
cover the smell of cooking, of sour body, of dead animal in the
sewer that stopped flowing every August. But I couldn't solve
it, and looked at Mama, watching anxiously, but she just smiled
and whispered do your best, and I did, but it never resolved, and
here are the roses I've heard so much about, the cup of tea on
the garden table, the radio muttering something about horses,
time slows and stops, and there's no point having any regrets
about where you held your foot, or how slippery the bar was
(the schematics hadn't mentioned that), or all of those equations
going to waste in a beautiful English summer garden. T (period
X) = I don't know, Mama, I don't, the linear equaliser where Lu
= 0 when u is unknown and L is the linear operator, Shana it can
be done but, the smell of apricot-coloured rose, of life, of love,
of the end of the small dreams we dared to dream sitting in our
house, listening to the sound of

Incident near Hoxtolgay Town

1   46°34'N 85°58'E

This occurred several summers ago somewhere between Hoxtolgay Town and Xazgat Town. I've only just got around to sitting down, finding paper, sharpening a pencil and writing. I'm no fan of writing. The moment you start, things stop happening; like they're ossified, made bone, like the dinosaurs in the desert outside Hoxtolgay. But that's for another time. The following occurred because of something (no one remembers what) Ganbold's father said to Khulan's father when they were both ambitious (and angry) young men.

Firstly, I'd like you to imagine the desert – sand on mudstone, or maybe siltstone (what am I saying, I know nothing about rocks), making layers that are themselves tilted, upended, deformed by time, exposing tears in the desert, each going down for miles. Some long, bedsheet tears, others more holes, all of them descending into the bowels of the Xinjiang Uygur Autonomous Region. As a boy, I was told to avoid the desert at night. One wrong step and I'd end up in London or Johannesburg or sitting miles down, broken bones, calling for help that'd never come because no one would ever hear me, slowly thirsting or starving to death. An image of terrors, of various Chinese hells, for a boy, but that's how it was.

Secondly, I'd like you to imagine layers of coal – the remains of ancient forests (hard to believe now, looking at the arid waste outside Hoxtolgay) – sitting miles below these tears. There'd been forests, jungles, strange red and yellow birds, long-extinct mammals with tusks and fangs, all of this. Imagine it if you can. And imagine this coal on fire. For although it was miles beneath the surface, it'd been burning for thousands of years. Just enough oxygen from the fissures to keep it going. Not that you'd know. Standing above one of these holes there was no heat, no lack of breathable air, no sulphur fumes. But according to the scientists it was all on fire. As a child, I found this difficult to understand. Who started the fire, and when? Someone must've, or were there other mechanisms? Did someone drop a cigarette? Or was it rising lava, causing the earth to collapse in nation-sized sinkholes?

Thirdly, imagine Ganbold standing beside one of the bigger openings. He's sixty, but looks older, grey hair, a prune face, flat nose with protruding bristles. Short, stooped, wandering to and fro, checking the hose, saying to himself, 'It's the persistence of such ideas that worries me most.' Ganbold used to be a jockey, a writer, a line-marker, a barman, a prison warden, many things. Not anymore. Now he can't remember his wife's name, his daughter's name, his son's name, anything much, although he can remember what he wrote. A story about a man in the desert who was paid by Khulan (the regional administrator) to supervise the watering, the dampening (it has many names) of the coal. Ganbold stands beside a fire-hose watching water flowing into the opening, down the sides, splashing and gurgling towards the coal seam. This, he's been told, will retard the fire. The government has tried mud-plugging, capping, in-filling, with no success. And this process is important (he's been told) because eventually the regional authorities may need to mine the coal to power boilers to make electricity. Once, hundreds of men, women and children stood beside hundreds of holes watching their hoses dampening the coal. Now, he's the only one left. Why, he's not sure. Maybe there's no more money to pay water-dampeners? Either way, here he is, in the desert, adjusting his hose, moving around the hole (as he's been trained to do), mumbling, '... *grey sand on mudstone, or maybe siltstone ...*' Sometimes he gets hot, wipes his forehead with a handkerchief that's been ironed by the woman with whom he lives, takes a drink from the bottle the same woman has sent, stares at the sun, returns to adjusting the hose, removing kinks, wondering why the flow is so slow.

Ganbold sees a man on a horse riding towards him, realises it's Supervisor Khulan, and wonders why today, why has he ridden out to see him today? A few minutes later, Khulan arrives, waves a few flies from his face (Ganbold doesn't bother with this anymore) and says, 'How's business?' Ganbold shrugs and says all's well, nothing to report, and Khulan gets down to business. He says, 'If you remember, Ganbold, we gave you a raise six months ago.' Ganbold thinks about this. Did they? A raise? How much? Maybe it's him, maybe he did get a raise, and maybe he seems ungrateful asking for more money (the strange woman in his house said he should). So he says, 'How much was I given?' Khulan says he was given a considerable amount, Ganbold asks how much, and Khulan (smiling) says, 'Well, if you can't remember, it's not my place to tell you.' Ganbold thinks this is fair. They can't be standing in the middle of the desert discussing confidential matters, and Khulan wouldn't have ridden all this way to tell him he'd just had a raise if he hadn't had a raise, therefore, he must have had a raise. So he says, 'I'm sorry I asked, Supervisor Khulan.' Khulan finds this amusing, grins, says, 'Sorry, what did you say your name was?'

Ganbold thinks and thinks but can't remember, and just says, 'I'm employee number 453, trained dampener, would you like to see my certificate?' Khulan says no, that won't be necessary. Just grinning. He asks him if he still makes love to his wife, but Ganbold says my wife, my wife? Do we? Do we make love, Supervisor Khulan? Khulan says yes, all the time, you make love all the time, you with your stubby willy, your wife with her little bosoms, and Ganbold smiles and says of course, of course, and because he wants to look busy, and not lose his job like the hundreds of others, he adjusts the hose that waters the coal in the desert outside Hoxtolgay Town.

2   和什托洛盖火车站

Now the story moves to Hoxtolgay Town itself. Just outside the main quarter, a warren of alleyways, small mud houses with flat roofs, children playing in the sun, clothes drying in the breeze, and here, follow me, inside one of the more solid, more substantial homes, stands twenty-six-year-old Delbee, a brown-haired, brown-eyed woman with a long and beautiful face. Like she's from some fairytale – smooth skin, red cheeks, fine lashes that her father, Supervisor Khulan, describes as feminine. Delbee is anxious, flustered, trying to find Jargal's socks, his underwear, the Nike T-shirt his grandmother (her mother) gave him last year as a going-away present (although they're only just going away now). She says to her son, 'Jargal, sit here now!' So the boy sits on the bed where his mother indicates. But all the time, he's jumpy, twitchy limbs, like he can't sit still no matter how hard he tries. Delbee says, 'And when we get there, no wandering!' She stands in front of her son with her hands on her hips, face set hard, like she means it, and Jargal stops twitching (for a moment), then she says, 'Got it?' He nods. She's never sure if he's understood, or just doesn't care. But this is Jargal. Delbee continues packing her son's bag (she's already packed her own) and says, 'If she thinks you're too much trouble she'll send you home, and then what would the journey through the desert have meant?' The boy says I'll be good, I'll behave, and she says, no wandering. I can't afford to lose you anywhere, especially the city, especially with millions of people around, I'll never see you again.

Delbee thinks about it. Should she? Should she attach his chain? She used to, up until age nine, ten, but then people (including her father) told her it was cruel, the boy (despite his condition) wasn't an animal, and she shouldn't do it. So now she doesn't (although she knows it would make her life easier). She says, 'What are you going to say to your aunt?' Jargal tries to remember; crosses his legs, squeezes them, rubs his face (and she stops him), making some of his usual guttural sounds, and says, 'Thanks for having me for the summer.' His mother says good, never forget your manners or she'll send you home and I won't be here to look after you, Jargal. He asks (for the hundredth time) where she'll be, and she says she has to find someone, another man, a father, someone with money, and she'll never find such a person in Hoxtolgay (which, she thinks, is only good for pigs and simpletons).

An hour later, Jargal's bag is packed, Jargal is dressed, they lock the door and walk towards the centre of town. Mrs Batbaatar asks where they're going and Delbee explains, Jargal is going to stay with his aunt in the city. Mrs Batbaatar says what a big adventure, I bet you're looking forward to it, Jargal? Mother and son continue through the maze of alleys, past spice-sellers, sheep brains and rugs, cardamom and Rolex watches, and Delbee says,

'You may have to stand in the train. But you can do that. If you need to, sleep on your rug. The main thing is, if the train stops don't get off, don't wander, you always wander.' The boy says not always, in fact, he hardly ever wanders, but she says, 'If you get off and the train leaves without you there won't be time for anyone to look for you.' She stops and turns, her son has gone, and she calls, 'Jargal?' Again! Now she's sure this journey was a bad idea. 'Jargal?' Then Mr Batbaatar (Mrs Batbaatar's husband) emerges from Farhadi alleyway with Jargal. He has him by the earlobe, and Jargal cowers with the pain of Mr Batbaatar's fingers. Mr B presents the boy, and shouts at him: 'Can't you think about your mother for once?' This time, Jargal is still, cowering, head down, like a dog that's just been kicked, but Mr B doesn't care. He's had enough of the boy, and seeing what he puts his mother through. If only he had a father to instil discipline. But that, he knows, the whole alleyway knows, is the point of Delbee's journey to the city. He says to the boy, 'Any more of this and you'll taste my boot again, got it?'

3 Back in the Gurbantünggüt Desert

Later the same afternoon, Ganbold is busy at work. The sun is at a strange, divergent angle to the earth, and Ganbold is wilting. No more food; no more water, and he can't drink from the hose as it's salty. He mentioned this to Supervisor Khulan, he said, 'What if I run out of water on a hot day?' Khulan laughed, patted his horse (whom he calls Ochirbat) and said, 'What, you'd have me install a swimming pool, a lake, a dam in the desert?' Yes, of course, Ganbold thought. What a ridiculous, an unreasonable request. A swimming pool? A lake? A dam? What would be the point of that? And anyway (as Khulan explained) it would evaporate within days, and then what would have been the point of spending millions making somewhere for him, the ungrateful Ganbold, to drink? So he apologised, said he can wait till he gets home, but Khulan told him he'd be docked a day's wage for showing disrespect to his supervisor. Ganbold said, 'Of course, entirely understandable.'

Ganbold adjusts the hose, peers down into the hole, wonders why it's only ever this hole, considering there are so many. Khulan has explained that, too: 'Our hydrology people have decided this hole is closest to the seam.' Ipso facto, the water, used here, would do the most good. Ganbold thinks and thinks, but the reason won't come to him, and he says, 'In the long day of the desert, he waits. According to the government, enough water and the seam will extinguish and there'll be enough coal for all future generations of northerners, and he, the dampener, will be remembered as the hero who stood here, day after day, while other men lived the high life.' He wonders if they'll put up a statue of him. If someone will write his biography (now he's no longer able to write his own). But all of this aside, he sees Supervisor Khulan coming towards him again, gets busy with his hose, tells himself not to complain about the water, puts on his shirt (the government has standards), looks up again and can't recognise Ochirbat, or Supervisor Khulan. Who is it? Just staring, watching, and now he drops the hose.

A boy. It's a boy. No older than eleven or twelve, and he comes closer, sucks on his hands, his fingers, his thumb, stops short of the hole and calls, 'Are you the railway man?' Ganbold says no, he's not the railway man, who's the railway man, and the boy says the man who tells the train when to go, are you him, and where is the train? Ganbold remembers his safety procedures (he had to complete a three week course). He says to the boy, 'Come no closer.' The boy isn't close, and isn't moving, but procedures need to be followed. Ganbold recites what he's memorised (quite a feat, considering): 'The Hoxtolgay Coal and Resource Initiative was started as an attempt ...' Wrong speech. What was it? Searches his brain cells: 'No one except authorised personnel may approach the seams. No one may look down, take photographs or film, throw objects into holes.' But the boy just asks which way the train went. Ganbold says which train, where, when, and the boy says the train to the city, the train taking him to his aunt to stay while his Mama looks for a man who might be his Papa, although do you think she'll find someone, do you think, sir? Ganbold doesn't understand. He says, 'You were on a train?' The boys jumps about and says yes, yes, the train, so you did see it! Ganbold says the tracks are miles away, beyond that valley, have you walked that far, son? The boy seems confused, crosses his legs again, bites his fingers again, says if my Mama finds a Papa I might have a brother. He takes a step forward, Ganbold tells him to take a step back, he stops and says, 'They went while I was peeing.' Ganbold thinks that makes sense, but he's hotter still, and woozy, feels himself falling, and a moment later he's on the ground and the boy's walking towards him, and he manages, 'Stop, you can't come any closer.' But the boy does, says can you take me back to the train, and Ganbold says I can't leave this position under any circumstances. You know what happens then? The boy says no, and Ganbold says that's a capital offence, and you've seen the men, haven't you, strung up in the market square.

A minute later, Ganbold feels better, and stands. He points to the mountains and says the train lies beyond those, the Hoxtolgay Mountains, and if you start walking now ... Although he's not sure that's the direction. He still feels woozy and sick in the guts, but he doesn't want the boy falling into a hole, because then he'd be in trouble, too, charged with not following safety procedures, and that, he knows, can end just as badly as leaving your position in the first place. So he points north to where he thinks the train is. Either way, there's no one around. If something happens to the boy, if he dies of thirst, if he falls into the burning coal, no one will be able to say it was his fault.

The boy is already wandering back across the desert. He stops, looks back at Ganbold, and Ganbold shoos him and says, 'Go on, keep walking, there's nothing for you here.'

4 The Clay Terraces

The next morning, Ganbold rests against a yardang. Picks at the shale and schist, remembers the lecture about coal, 30 billion metric tonnes burning beneath his arse. *And if he's the one who saves it all* ... He might, he will, Khulan has told him, describing the parades in his honour, the stamps with his face, the Mighty Leader coming to Hoxtolgay to thank him personally. He's said all of this, shaken his hand, thanked him. This has elicited a certain *glow* in the old man; a certain pride, like in the old days, when he led a road-marking team in the north of Dzungaria. Nation-building days, when a man knew his worth, and was rewarded. But things (he senses) are different now. Where are the miners? The diggers? The power stations? The freeways? The Great Leaps Forward into a future of stainless steel sinks and three-wheeled cars?

Ganbold sits in the shade of the ship-shaped terraces, aberrations of uni-directional winds that have been criss-crossing the desert for millions of years, peeling skin and silica from man, frog, rock. When he got home from work the previous evening he decided not to mention the boy to the woman with whom he lives. He's not sure if she's reliable. He suspects she's been telling Supervisor Khulan all of the things he tells her. Maybe she's even a spy, planted in his house to make sure he's doing his job properly. Yes, that's the most likely explanation. A spy. But the incident did stay on his mind. When he went to bed, when he tried to get to sleep, all he could see was the boy; when the crowd ran past his window, when the lanterns flashed, when the voices raised in alarm, when the calls went out for a search party, all he could think of was the boy. Did he follow the correct procedure? Is there a procedure for lost children? Either way, he probably made it back to the train. It's unlikely he would've fallen into a hole. So here he is now, on a much cooler day, watching the water pour into the hole, imagining each drop quenching the coal.

'Ganbold!' He looks up, sees Supervisor Khulan riding towards him, and behind him, five or six other men on horses. He picks up the hose, moves it, and when Khulan arrives he says, 'It's been a busy morning, Supervisor. I realised I'd been given a raise after all, and it was ungrateful of me to ask for more money, so I hope the committee might overlook this.' Khulan says, 'Stop babbling, Ganbold. Tell me, have you seen a boy go past?' Ganbold knows he needs to be careful. If there is a policy about lost boys, and he hasn't followed it, this may not end well. So he says, 'A boy? What sort of boy?' Khulan says for god sake, what does it matter what sort of boy, a boy, there aren't many boys in the desert, are there? Ganbold has to agree, but realises he can't say this. So he says, 'What time would the boy have passed?' Khulan says what's it matter what time the boy passed, either you saw him or you didn't. Ganbold, thinking, and he says I'm trying to remember, and Khulan says you old fool, and he and the party start riding off, but Ganbold realises that if they do find the boy, and the boy says he saw an old man in the desert dampening the coal, and since he's the last remaining dampener, this wouldn't end well for him. So as they ride off, Ganbold calls, 'A boy?' They stop, return, and Khulan says can you remember? Ganbold waits, then says, 'They told me, for this job, it didn't matter … a monkey could do it. Who said that, Supervisor?' Khulan knows it was him. His idea. To put the old fool in the desert, never pay him a cent, and he'd never realise what a pointless job he had, what a pointless life he'd led, just standing there, watering the desert. So Ganbold decides, points south to the river, and says, 'The boy went that way.'

Violettowne

1.

This might be about what Bert Billingsworth did to Tho. North's youngest brother, or George Ley's cousin, who knows, but the Honourable told me to write down as much as I could remember. The Honourable said every detail, every bit, don't skimp, it'll all help, it might save your life Ivan. So I'll start by saying this happened in Violettowne and Violettowne is a rough raw uncivilised place and there's not much there apart from pigs and horses. Straight to the story, and it was 3.15 I think, perhaps later, but I've already told the police that. Me the police too, but not now. Either way, I was left to watch George Ley, who was locked up for hitting his wife, and Thomas North, who'd stolen a sack of grain. Bert Billingsworth was in the cell with them in Violettowne, with its one street and public house, its gaol made of big granite blocks. Bert was in for vagrancy. He never done nothing wrong much and probably shouldn't have been there, but he was and it was 3.15 or maybe 3.30 I don't know as I was sleeping, and I was woken by a drama in the cells, a lot of moving about and huffing and heaving and I shot up and said oi, what are you lot up to? No reply, so I turned up the gas and there's Tom, and there's George, and there's Bert lying on the ground, and I said what have you done to him? George shrugged and lit a cigarette. Thomas laid down to sleep. So I opened the cell, shook Bert, but there are no words or him moving, just nothing, and he's dead, I'm sure he's dead, and I said what did you dogs do to him?

2.

The Honourable Nicholas Hannen was the one who passed the sentence that wasn't a sentence and according to the even more Honourable I shoulda knowed that and not did what I did. So back in Violettowne the doctor in the dock said oh, yes, he died from a blow to the head, and it's simple, open and closed, someone, one man killed him. And me thinking I shoulda been awake, I shoulda seen, I shoulda known what was going on, but anyway, the reason why I'm writing for my life isn't because I fell asleep that night, no, it's because I did what no other man would do, and it was right and proper and I have no regrets. Mr Hannen got George up and said what happened and George said not sure, I was sleeping, and I woke, and Tom was standing with the hammer in his hand, and the judge wanted to know where the hammer come from, and I said (later, when it was my turn), I don't know, I can't remember no hammer. But it was still my fault. But I'm not writing for my life because of no hammer, no, nothing like that. Then Tho. North got up and he said he was shocked when he woke and saw George Ley standing above Bert Billingsworth with a hammer in *his* hand. That's what he said, and during all this George looked at Tom and said you liar, and Tom looked back and said the same thing, and they tried to get at each other but me, Ivan, Ivan Samson, me and the other men held them back so that couldn't happen. Then the Honourable summoned me and said what had happened and I said I didn't know, I was busy in the armoury and I didn't see, I should've I suppose but I didn't. He called me unreliable and simple and I said so be it.

3.

Too much for a simple man like me, which is why the decision fell to the Honourable, who sat for days in his office and although

I was a witness I still had to bring him tea and toast and he kept asking me questions and I told him what I knew (apart from the falling asleep) and in the end he just shrugged and said well, there's nothing for it. So I was sent to summon the people and the Honourable got up and said if neither of you will say then I have no choice but to find you both guilty of murdering Albert Billingsworth. Then Tom and George are calling out it couldn't have been both of us but the Honourable said what else can I do, and if that's the game you want to play. The lawyermen argued there's no precedent, it can't be done, only one man can be found guilty of one crime, but the Honourable shooshed them and said so what, get my cart, Mr Samson, I want to get out of this pigshit town. George shouting no it wasn't him, and Tom saying you rotten liar, and me and the men dragging them back to their cells.

4.

It ended at the gallows. It always ends at the gallows. Both men standing side by side, George pissing himself, but that didn't mean he was innocent, or guilty. I said time's up, gents. Take a look. And they looked at each other. Can't someone decide, now, to speak up. Who killed Bert? The same shouting and struggling but we had them tied good by then. I said come on now, it's time, one of you. I was sure one would break. Even the innocent man might decide to die for the other. But no, shouting and screaming and I lost patience and held the lever in my hand and said if this is what's writ, and no other man in his high and mighty will agree to do it, then I have no choice but to carry out the Honourable's sentence. So, of course, you know what I did. But I have to make it clear before the sun rises one last time over Violettowne.

The death of Tomas Kirja

Book I

I write this thirty-eight years after the death of Tomas Kirja, to remind people – no, to *tell* people – about Tomas, and the years XX34 to X176. Not that I was alive for all of that time, but I was told, heard stories, saw pictures (most of which have now gone). I became fascinated by Tomas's story but, regretfully, failed to meet him by seven years. As you'll see, this story ends with a suicide. Not some sort of dramatic event; more, a suicide of necessity, of neatness. Tomas's life had become a collection of loose ends. Most of these had to do with books. There was a time when books were everywhere, and that nearly happened again in the Kirja era. Bookshops sold books; libraries kept thousands, and people borrowed them, took them home, spent (sometimes) weeks reading them. Poor old Tomas, and his love of books. Story goes, he filled his bedroom with them, couldn't sleep without them; was always quoting lines from them, so that sometimes you couldn't tell what was Tomas and what was (say) Ernest Hemingway.

So this is how it all started.

In XX34 Tomas received a letter from a lawyer telling him his uncle, George, had died, and left him a collection of books. This didn't interest Tomas because he was a more practical type, employed by the government to carry out building inspections, write engineering reports – things like bridges and fords. He lived with his mother; he'd always lived with his mother. He'd never (so it was said) had any sort of long-term relationship with a woman. A pity, I was told (by his great-nephew), because Tomas was a decent man, caring, considerate, but perhaps too predictable, too conservative, not up to taking risks. Either way, Tomas received the letter, and wrote back asking for more information. This is the reply he received:

Dear Mr Kirja

Your uncle held a collection of 623,130 books. All of these were (and are) kept in his house. The hallways (see attached photos) are crowded, and there's little ease of movement. I've been told that your uncle had some sort of compulsive disorder, and couldn't help but buy books. Apparently, in the end, he was unable to show people his books, in case someone asked to borrow one. If you could give me instructions before 5 July XX34 I will be able to plan for the disposal, movement or storage of these volumes.

On and on like this. So Tomas wrote back and said he had no interest in books, and could they be sold, and the money forwarded to him? The lawyer said this wasn't his job, and you (Tomas) can arrange to have it done at your own cost, but again, could you let me know by the agreed date.

This made Tomas angry. He hadn't asked for the letter, for the books, for his uncle to die. He was just about to write back to the lawyer and tell him he didn't want any part of his uncle's estate, when his mother said, 'Georgetown? That's not far. Why don't we drive out there next Sunday and take a look?' Tomas couldn't argue with his mother. So they drove to his uncle's house, the lawyer let them in and they inspected the forest, the tonnes, the avalanche-in-waiting of books that lined every wall, every inch of floor, the toilet, laundry, under the bed, over the bed, in the bed.

His mother said, 'The lot of it, rubbish!' She said to the lawyer, 'Get rid of it, burn it, all of it.' But he said, 'That might cost a lot of money.' As they discussed this, Tomas stood in the corner of the living room leafing through a book called *Istoria e dimostraziono*, by someone called Galileo. He became intrigued by the drawings of planets and stars, and arrows and lines showing how they moved. This appealed to his rational side, his engineer's temperament. He tried to read the text, but it was in some strange language, and he said to the lawyer, 'Do you think he kept a copy in English?'

'Perhaps.' (Guessing this was a good sign).

So the lawyer and Tomas (as Tomas's mother shouted at them to stop being so stupid) searched the piles of books, but couldn't find anything else by Galileo. It didn't matter. Tomas soon found a book called *Winnie the Pooh*. Although it wasn't so technical, it was intriguing. Stories about anthropomorphic creatures running around the countryside. He said to his mother, 'Isn't this charming?' He showed her. She said, 'We're not here to play. We're here to make a decision.'

So, for the sake of brevity I'll skip the next twelve months. Suffice to say, Tomas went home, thought about these books and decided there must be more to them than paper, ink, charming drawings, photographs of cars, pictures of naked women reclining in gardens (his uncle had a room full of these). He wondered whether the sort of society he lived in, he'd been brought up in, might benefit from books. After all, there were so many problems that didn't have answers. Why, for example, people had stopped talking to each other. Why politicians lived in walled villages, eating food cooked by slaves. Why 32% of the population committed suicide before thirty. Maybe, he wondered, the solutions were in the millions of pages he'd seen in his uncle's house, and if this were the case, what a tragedy it would be to throw them all away, put them on a pile, burn them (one book, he'd noticed, had showed this being done in a country named Germany).

One day, Tomas decided. He told his mother he'd rented a warehouse, and decided to move all of the books. She said, 'Why?' He said, 'I'm not sure, but I think books might be valuable.' She said, 'But they're made from paper. They're falling apart. They've been eaten by mould. They're written in languages no one understands anymore.' He said, 'I just have a hunch.' She said, 'What is this hunch?' He told her about more of the books he'd gathered, brought home, attempted to study, to *read*, to make sense of. 'For example,' he told her, 'this one' – showing her – 'is about Turkie.'

'Turkie?'

Reading the gold letters: '*The Navigations, Peregrinations and Voyages made into Turkie*, by Nicolas de Nicolay. This country must have been amazing. Houses, crowded together, the smell of burning incense, lamb roasting on spits, men singing from towers called minarets.'

'Minarets?'

'Attached to mosques, where people worshipped gods. Prayers, five times a day, and if you committed a crime, off with your head.' Showing her what this might look like.

'They cut off people's heads?'

'If you broke the law. The Eye had nothing to do with it. Apparently everything was decided by wise old men and women.'

She didn't get this at all, but she did say, 'Maybe these books *are* worth reading?'

'That's why I've rented the warehouse. And arranged for the books to be moved.'

'How much will it cost?'

'Don't worry. I'll offset it with the price of a library membership.'

His mother didn't understand. 'On your own head. But don't come running to me when you lose all of your money.'

Because (and don't forget, I wasn't there at the time), Tomas had decided to make something he'd read about. It was called a library. There'd been at least one of these, in a place called Babel, because he'd read about it in a book by a man named Borges. Borges had described a place with endless volumes, arranged randomly, but (and here was the exciting thing) if these books could be ordered, catalogued, made sense of, the whole world might be understood. As far as Tomas could tell, this had never happened in Borges's time but, he figured, maybe it could happen now. Just think, he told his mother, later that night, everything explained.

'What needs explaining?'

'Why people used to live in *neighbourhoods*. Why they had *hospitals*, run by *governments*. There must be something behind these ideas, don't you agree?'

Tomas spent weeks preparing his warehouse. He used Borges's story as a guide, constructing shelves for the books. He installed skylights so people could read. People. Because his library would function this way. Not by him alone having access to all of the books (how could one mind make sense of all that history?), but by allowing people to share his collection. So, a citizen would buy a share (say, for one dollar) and this would allow them access, any time of day or night, to the *entire* collection. Then, *then*, this collective brain would understand the whole universe (as described in *The Wonderful Wizard of Oz*). People would get together, discuss these ideas, work out how society might be improved (by reference to history), form groups and enact these changes. For example, he told his mother, this book about Italian cooking.

'Italian?'

'Wheat used to make pasta, which is boiled, covered with a sauce, and eaten. Simple. Apparently full of flavour. We could have cooking classes, and people interested in the *rec-i-pes* could relearn the art of Italian cooking.'

'Why?'

'Why not? Or macramé. Weaving string to make pot holders. Or dreamcatchers.'

'What are they?'

'They had the ability to catch dreams, hold them, and make them available for later use. Who'd have guessed? Reusable dreams! And what about this one?' Showing her *Alice's Adventures in Wonderland*. 'Children that could be shrunk, put down a hole, meet rabbits. What a restrictive world we live in.'

Moving day, or days. Seventeen trucks in a convoy, driving between his uncle's house and his warehouse. Each book placed into a nylex bag with fifty others. Dropped onto pallets. Unloaded with forklifts. A marvel, because no one had worked out how to fix forklifts since the Great Dumbing. So, instead of millions of abandoned forklifts sitting around, now, with the help of a book called *Service and Repairs DX345 Forklift*, they could be *fixed*, kept in working order. There, in itself, is an idea worth millions, he told his mother.

On a cold, rainy morning, Tomas opened the door to his warehouse and surveyed his books. Thousands of bags. He'd asked a few workmates to help. He'd said, 'If you're free on the weekend, I'd appreciate the company.' But when he explained, it was always, 'Ah, I think I'm busy with the football procedure.'

'An hour?'

'You know what happens if your kids don't kick the ball, Tomas. If they don't do the procedure.'

Tomas had to agree. The penalties were severe.

His mother couldn't come. She was busy with Italian cooking. But he did have one friend, Romeo, who said he could spare a few hours.

Book II

Those were better times. When Tomas Kirja still had hope. That his library would be sorted, patronised, enjoyed; that it would change people's lives, make them *happy*, make them think, lead to useful social changes. People would fulfil their ('God given') potential. Order would be restored to a chaotic universe courtesy of the 'Dewey' system (named in honour of a grandson of the philosopher Scrooge McDuck). Nature would be restored (he'd put aside dozens of shelves for 580-590).

For the first week, Tomas and Romeo sat, surrounded by books, attaching labels. Every hour or so, Romeo would take a box of sorted books, climb one of the ladders around the warehouse, find the correct shelf and insert the book. Then he'd return to Tomas and say, 'This might take some time.'

Tomas would say, 'It'll take as long as it takes.'

Romeo didn't like this at all. He was using his personal leave, and was he, Tomas, going to reimburse him? No. This obsessive engineer, sitting on the cold floor in shorts and socks and slippers, looking through another book. 'This one here, Romeo. *The Voyage of the Beagle*, by Charles Darwin. He was the one who came up with the idea of natural selection.'

'But the Eye says ...'

'No. See, my point. We've been lied to. I think this is what happened. After the revolution, after books were gotten rid of, people *forgot*. How things were. Where they'd started. What they meant. They forgot. And because they forgot ...' Opening his hands out, like he was saying, This is what we're left with.

'Even so,' Romeo said, 'what can *we* do about it?'

'We can sort, that's what we can do. We can shelve. We can *read*.'

So they kept at it. Romeo said he had to return to work, but Tomas said, 'When the history of the world's at stake?' So Romeo took off another week, and another, and they continued sorting. One day, as they sat labelling, Romeo said, 'What about your job as an engineer?'

'Forget it,' Tomas replied. 'They sacked me.' Although he didn't seem to care.

'Why?'

'I used up my leave, I didn't go in, I didn't call – I don't even care, Romeo.' Explaining how he though there was more to it.

'Why?'

'Word's got out, what we're doing. Certain powers aren't happy.' Tapping the side of his nose.

'Which powers?'

'Don't worry. It's all under control.' Although Tomas had seen the signs. The locks, tampered; the small, hidden cameras in the bathroom (he hadn't found them, but guessed they were there); the phone calls at three am, with no one on the other end.

'You mean we're being watched?'

'Possibly.'

This was enough for Romeo. He'd already used up all of his leave, and he had a wife and four children. As much as he agreed with Tomas, and as much as he'd grown fond of sitting reading about Christopher Columbus and Isaac Newton, he couldn't risk it any more. So the next morning when Tomas arrived at the warehouse, Romeo wasn't there. Just a note under the door saying, 'I wish you all the best, Tomas. If anyone can see it through, you can. Your friend, Romeo. PS, I took that book about Bertrand Russell.'

Tomas didn't care. He just went in, sat down, and kept labelling.

That night, sitting around the table, eating lasagne, Tomas did the maths. He worked out that it would take another ninety-three years to finish his labelling, his shelving. Then the cataloguing. Another thirty years, perhaps, to make detailed notes, index cards, come up with a system to make sense of the books, the words in them, the world. A problem. Because he was already sixty-three and the average male lifespan was 143. Not enough. Maybe he could open the library, find someone to take over, complete what Librarian Borges had begun. Maybe he'd meet a nice woman and she'd fall pregnant, they'd have children and these, generations of them, could finish the job. Nothing was out of the question.

'When will you be finished with those books?' his mother asked.

'Soon.'

'We're running out of savings.'

'When we open, and I charge for admission, millions will come. We'll be rich.'

She didn't believe anything he said any more. She wondered what he did all day in his warehouse. He couldn't tell her that the real problem was that he'd come to love books, and spent most of his time reading them, so that some days he only got two or three labelled, some weeks, a dozen shelved. Hundreds of years, millennia, before it was finished.

Book III

Then things got worse. Word got around about Tomas, and his warehouse, his inheritance, and his obsession. As it turned out, other people had books. Although it had been a long time since any were published, the thing was, they'd lasted, sometimes for thousands of years. So when Tomas arrived at his warehouse every morning there were more books. Donations, with little notes attached: 'I found these in my great-grandmother's basement and heard you were the book man.' Some mornings there would be ten boxes, another hundred books to add to his collection. Of course, he couldn't get rid of them, or refuse donations. That way, he might be missing part of the picture Borges had described. For instance, he'd found a book on something called insects. Insects were small animals, often too small to see, but they'd had an important job pollinating plants (don't ask). As another example, *Moby Dick*, a story about a giant whale. This explained fish, and candle fat, and lighting, and Shakespeare [890] writing 'plays' at night in the taverns he stayed in. It explained the Great Fire of London, and references in the Bible [200] to someone called Jonah being eaten alive. See, Tomas tried to tell his mother. All of this knowledge links together, and then you understand.

'What?'

'The world.'

'I understand the world, and all of the bills I pay, with no help from you!'

So Tomas laboured on. Another year, two, five, ten. By this point he had thousands, hundreds of thousands more books

than he'd started with. He re-did the maths and worked out that this job would take him another two thousand years. Then more books. Five thousand. As every day, more volumes arrived. And one day, he came home and his mother was dead. Lying on the ground, a copy of *Macbeth* in her hand. This made him feel better. Deep down, he hoped, standing at her funeral, she understood his mission, and its importance. If only she'd said this to him.

Word got around. Instead of spies watching him, he now had politicians, celebrities, movie stars coming to visit him. Mainly to build their image as deep thinkers, thoughtful, intelligent. They'd bring a film crew, and peruse his not-very-full shelves, and say things to him like, 'All the knowledge of the world. What do you make of it?'

'Nothing yet. I still haven't organised it. One day, when I get the chance to read all of these books ...'

'When will that be?'

'I can't rush. I have to get it right. The future of the world depends upon it.'

Then they'd go away, and show this footage to their followers, with comments like 'TODAY I MET A PROFOUNDLY WISE MAN.'

This led to more books, and more mountains of knowledge. Tomas rented another warehouse, and another, and filled them with books. He hired people to help him label them, but mostly, these people were idiots, put the books on the wrong shelves, and he had to go back and fix their mistakes. So he got rid of them all. That would be quicker.

By the time he was a hundred and ten, Tomas had seven warehouses full of books. But every day he'd get up, eat a can of beans (grown using 'Bean Growth and Development in the Tropics'), go to his original warehouse and sort books. There'd

be a line of people at the door offering to help, but he'd say
no. There'd be more academics and celebrities, and he'd say,
'I haven't got time for all of that anymore.' Seeing how, like
Borges, he was slowly going blind, losing the ability to examine
each book, marvel at its wonders. Add the label, shelve it. This
was his life, his joy, his purpose. Smelling the acid-eaten pages,
feeling the rough paper, and saying to himself, 'If only I had
another hundred years.'

Then, something even worse happened. People started
approaching him on the street and asking advice. He was the
wisest man alive; he was a sort of book god; he had the answer
to everything, neatly shelved in his brain. They'd say, 'Tomas,
tell us, why is it that the world has been at war for seven hundred
years?' At first, he would give them some answer. He'd say, 'It is
in man's brain, his heart, his soul. It's in his nature to fight.' Or
they might ask: 'Why are there no bees?' And he'd say, 'Because
we prefer plastic over plants.'

Tomas didn't like this at all. People phoning him with
questions; slipping them under his door; printing Tomas Kirja
T-shirts and making posters with quotes (he couldn't remember
saying). 'I never asked for any of this,' he said to a woman who
came to his door one night needing to know why her daughter
wouldn't speak to her. 'I don't know any more than you, or
anyone. I just sort the books.' Then she said, 'If you don't know,
who does?' And he replied, 'You. All of you.'

She didn't get this, and left.

'When the library opens,' he called after her, 'you can read
about it. Three hundred, Social Sciences. Or maybe 210:
Philosophy.'

He thought it neat how the world was summarised in ninety-
nine categories. How this system was so complete, and sensible.

If the world could be inserted into a library, as Borges had suggested, human ignorance could be eliminated. But of course, this could never happen. For one, he was nearly blind; and two, people only wanted to know what they already knew. Three, he didn't have thousands more years, and there was no one, really, who understood what he was trying to do.

So, one night, sitting at home with his beans (according to the coroner's report), he wrote a note explaining his dilemma, dressed in his old engineer's suit, walked all the way to warehouse number one and went in. The lights clunked on, revealing the half-full shelves. He called, 'Is anyone here?' And his voiced disappeared, smothered by tonnes of paper. He went to the middle of the room and sat on an old chair that had been his mother's. He thought it sad, how he'd spent so long as an engineer. Those years could've been another thousand volumes. He opened a bottle of old scotch, took a swig, and gazed up into the skylights. The moon, the stars that would keep appearing, according to what Galileo had told him, all those years ago. He smiled. He took a box of matches from his jacket pocket, lit one, leaned over and touched the flame to *The Historie of the World*, by Plinius Secundus. A moment later the fire spread. An alarm sounded, but the sprinklers didn't switch on. He'd made sure of that. A minute later the flames were licking at Metaphysics [110], then his own feet. But he didn't move. He just drank, and smiled, and said, 'It was inevitable, I guess.'

Box of bones

Yes, I've let the place go, but I'll explain. How we last had stock somewhere around, what was it, eighty-five, eighty-six? How, after that, the yards fell apart (what was the point of welding anything?). Overgrown with weeds. So that the productive part of our station ('Trenwood') became febrile, diseased, no longer up to it. But by then it didn't matter, because Mum and Dad had gone, Pop, the lot of them. Just me, and I had no desire to farm. The two thousand head of shorthorn, as it'd once been. No desire to hire help, muster twice a year, organise the freight. Make money. What for?

Then the house. Old. Walls cracked. The screen door banging in the breeze on long, hot afternoons full of flyspeck and the remains of roast beef. Shadows from the pepper tree moving across the porch. In my front window, on my bed, my body twisting like the seized-up cattle crush. Bare boards, worn to the lignin, the old rugs threaded and still sitting (full of mice) in the laundry. See, my world. A kitchen of dreams, cookbooks, recipes I've never made. Nice, how sweet and sour looks in the pictures, although there's always a missing ingredient. So it's just the same muffins, and dumplings, and pork, when we had a few pigs.

Me, sitting in my armchair, reading (over and over) what Dad wrote, of what he remembered. Starting with the blocky letters: 'Summer of 1934'. Although he may have been wrong – more like 1935? Dad was always precise. He had to be. If he was hiring men for the muster, or trucks, or horses to drive the mob, vaccines, food, even. See, anything you needed to stay alive, to stay in business, when you lived nine hundred miles from the nearest shop. There was no room for error. Everything had to be added up, divided, over-estimated. But let's just say it happened in 1934.

What? Wait. I'm going to tell you. Thirty years of thinking about it, and I've finally picked up a pen, sat down, and started writing. Which is hard. To work out what to say, the words in order, not giving too much or little away. And the question, always the question, about whether there's any point writing things down. Who cares what I've got to say? I'm the end of the line, no sons or daughters or cousins (sorry, there's Max, but he's off with the fairies). The point? Maybe I'm only writing for my own sake? Perhaps that's the only reason people write? You, my audience of zero, can go to hell.

So here I am, sitting at the old dining table where I scratched my name as a kid, and Dad belted me, and Mum stood and said, 'He didn't know.' A life of scratches and tears and old lino. Still there. Where you come in from the kitchen, settle in the old lounge, and look across at the box of bones.

You, my non-readers, are probably asking why I keep them in the lounge. I couldn't really say. They've been there for years – since the stock agent brought them in from the desert, all dingo-eaten, sun-dried and clunkety, even then (it had been eighteen months, and no one had found them, and they'd given up). This collection of bones gathered from the hottest, most distant part of the desert (still our land). Scattered (the agent said) over a square mile by wind, animals, time. This collection of bones I've looked at every day, for all those years. The big ones, and little ones, which is sad. He might have grown up to be an explorer, an engineer, a farmer.

So I write. About this story that defined my family, that haunted it, destroyed it, perhaps (although maybe that's too dramatic). This story of Pop, setting out in his old Dodge utility one Sunday morning in 1934. Kissing Nan on the cheek (perhaps, I wasn't there), ruffling Dad's hair and saying, 'I'll be back by three tomorrow.'

Because that's generally how long the trip took. A bore run – a journey of three hundred miles, stopping every half hour to check the dams, the hoses, the pumps, the windmills, the troughs – to make sure water was still flowing, animals still drinking. So long that Pop (who often took Dad) had to stop and sleep the night in the western districts. His old swag, still in the shed, under the billion or so stars we've owned for years.

So there's Pop, loading his swag, water, the trough brush, the tools he'd need to fix the windmills. There he is, smiling, laughing, exploring the food Nan had packed him. He liked to go, I guess – getting away from the house which, although big, was small in the scheme of the desert, and the land, and the sky that went from one horizon to the other. Liked being by himself, perhaps. His thoughts. His few books (still in the bookshelf, although ruined by sun and sand).

Pop points his ute in the right direction and sets off. Almost gets bogged before he's through the gate. Waves back to Nan and Dad, who's swinging circles from the porch post, whistling, asking his mum what's for tea (her saying, 'Only ever think of your stomach').

Pop driving for three hours, stopping to fill the tank from jerry cans, to check a few bores, tighten nuts and bolts and blades, watch some of the cattle grazing the sparse grasses – hardly any protein, although enough to keep the few animals going.

Meanwhile, Dad (my dad) wandering the sheds and yards,

up the hill, where four generations are buried, and where the Norwegian woman would be too, her grave still unmarked to this day. Reading the inscriptions on the headstones (all of which had been fetched from town) about 'Here sleeps blah blah' and 'In the Arms of God ...' Names and dates that probably meant nothing to him. Although he used to tell me that's all he'd do – wander. Climb the piles of old tyres, saw bits of wood and hammer them together. As Pop drove towards Bore No. 47; hoping his old Dodge would make it, his fuel pump would hold out, that he wouldn't blow more than two tyres. If he did, it was a long walk back. And even with plenty of water, in that heat, it would take some doing. Some surviving. So you just crossed your fingers and hoped for the best.

Maybe he stopped at the Wilga Caves, with their sooty ceilings and rock paintings. Lots of people did. Drove this far out just to see some scribbled emus and roos, hand splatters. Not much. I saw them once, never bothered again. But as you'll soon see, people came from all over to have a look. London, South Africa, Norway. Fancy that. From all the fjords and icebergs to Trenwood, just to see some crayon marks.

Pop drove for another hour, then staring into the distance, squinted to see two indistinct shapes. *No.* Surely not. Cattle perhaps? But as he got closer he knew. A kid, a boy, nine or ten, on his knees in the sand. And in front of him, a woman, lying, barely moving. This whole drama taking place beside a car. A car that wasn't up to the job. A city car, with white tyres and chrome and a radio, but not one meant for cattle country. Anyway, that car's still there today. Same spot. No glass or tyres or anything, just a rusted-out shell, and the birds and dingoes breeding and sleeping or using the shade. This old monument to what happened that day.

Pop pulls up and surveys the situation and this boy runs over to him and starts jabbering in some language he doesn't understand (Norwegian, but you've probably worked that out by now). The boy pulls at his sleeve and says, 'Mor, Mor,' and points to this woman, who Pop assumes (I assume) is the boy's mother. Pop goes over and kneels and sees the woman is dehydrated, barely breathing, hot all over. He says, 'Where's your water?' but the boy doesn't understand. Pop says, '*Water?*' and shows what he means with a pantomime, but the boy just stands there, confused.

Pop checked their car. Yes, there was a water container, but it was empty. And yes, the car was bogged, up to its axles. Pop quickly understood all this, but didn't understand what they were doing so far from anywhere, on the arse end of his property. 'What yers doing here?'

'Mor!'

'More what?'

The kid didn't make sense, so Pop pushed him away, went to the old Dodge, got some water and brought it over to the woman. He raised her, placed her body against his lifted knee and tried to give her a drink. But the water just ran out of her mouth, down her chin, onto her clothes (which were unsuitable too). He tried for five minutes, but the woman was past drinking, past talking. Pop thought, This won't end well. He knew when people were too far gone. He'd seen it, not just with stock, but with a man who'd worked for them, and wandered off and got lost after his wife had left him.

The boy was distraught, shouting, then sobbing. By now Pop'd had enough and told him to shut up, and he seemed to understand this, and was quiet for a minute as Pop thought what to do. There was no time to dig the car out. No point. So he dragged the woman to his ute, lifted her onto the tray, told the boy to sit beside her. Which he did. As they drove towards Trenwood for an hour, two, perhaps more, before the boy started hammering on the cab window, and Pop stopped and got out and checked the woman and could see that she was dead. But tried her pulse, and got onto the tray and breathed into her mouth (as the boy sat in a corner crying), and pumped her heart like he'd been told by the Flying Doctor, and eventually turned to the boy and said, 'It's too late, son.'

No reply.

'Your mum's dead.'

Nothing.

Pop wondered what to do. Go back? Bury her? Go home? Yes, that's all he could do. Go home. And if one of the windmills wasn't working, and his stock died because he hadn't got to check, then it would be this dead woman's fault. For driving into the desert, unprepared, and getting bogged, and making her problem his. He felt annoyed about this. Okay, she was dead, and that was a shame (especially for the kid), but some people refused to think things through, plan, consider how their actions might impact others.

Driving towards Trenwood with the boy beside him, his mum rattling around in the back of the ute, Pop said, 'Where you from?'

The boy said a few words, then settled.

Christ, Pop might've thought. What am I gonna do with this one?

Then the boy produced a newspaper clipping, with pictures of the caves and the Aboriginal paintings, and pointed them out, and said, '*Ab-o-rig-i-ne.*'

'You were going to look at them?' Indicating.

The boy didn't respond. Just bit his lip.

'What, yer mum's – she is yer mum? – she's some sort of scientist?'

The boy shook his head, reclaimed the cutting, folded it and put it in his pocket. Then he said a few sentences, finishing with the word *far*.

'Eh?'

'Far!' Using his own hands to show what might have been a bird flying through the desert, or a dunnart, tunnelling.

'What, you've come far? To see the caves? Well, they're on my property, and yer meant to write to me first, let people know – you know, the police? Did your mum contact the police? *The police?* Did she tell anyone she was coming?'

No response. Although, for the next hour, as they drove, the boy kept repeating himself, and this word, refining his pantomime, slowly becoming more agitated, at one point grabbing the wheel of the Dodge and trying to turn it around. Pop said, 'No, don't, you'll get us bogged, then we'll all end up ...'

Until sometime later, Pop drove into Trenwood, and Nan and Dad came running out, saw the woman in the ute, the boy, and started asking all sorts of questions. Pop told them what had happened, but that he couldn't make any sense of what this boy was saying.

So Nan had a turn. She took the boy in, settled him at the table with a glass of barley water, and said, 'What's your name?'

Just harsh words, glued together with phlegm. No one could understand a word. Nan said to Pop, 'What language is it, do you reckon?'

'Dunno. Wog?'

'He's not Italian. *Are you Italian, son? What's your name?*'

The boy was tired. He drank, but then fell asleep at the table, and Nan carried him into Dad's bed. Laid him out, and let him sleep.

Meanwhile, Pop took the woman from the Dodge, laid her on the porch and called to Nan: 'What should we do with her?'

Nan examined the woman, said how pretty she was, or had been, and how it was a shame, wasn't it, she was dead. Pop said it was her own fault. Fancy coming all this way with so little water. They knew she'd quickly turn, so they decided to put her in a stock trough, fill it, let the water keep her cold for now. Maybe, later, some relatives would want to claim her.

The boy slept through the afternoon. Nan tried to wake him when they had tea, but he just stirred, mumbled, continued sleeping. Dad said he watched him for a while, the way he slept with his mouth open, how his nostrils flared, his eyes flickered like a couple of mixy rabbits. Where, he wondered, had he come from? There were no signs. Just pale skin, burned around the edges, and hair so blond it was probably bleached. Then he felt in the boy's pockets and found a bus ticket, a comb, a half page of writing in this strange language. He had an encyclopedia, so he looked up a map of Europe, but this didn't help. He read a few of the words on the paper: '... vikingene reiste til England ...' But he wasn't sure. Was this some sort of small Viking, washed up on distant shores?

Then, just as they were getting ready for bed, the boy appeared in the doorway to the kitchen. He studied them, trying, perhaps, to remember where he was, what had happened. Nan said, 'Come over here, sit down, we've got some food for you.'

But he just started talking, and then shouting: 'Min far gikk der andre veien ...'

'Over here, son. We have beef ... you like beef?'

'*Lytte!*'

Pop shepherded him towards the table, sat him down, but he just ranted. He pointed to Pop, then Dad, as if to explain. He stood, walked around the room, pretended to search for something.

Nan placed the dish of food in front of him and said, 'Eat up. You'll feel better.'

The boy took the piece of paper I'd put back in his pocket, searched for a pen and started drawing. Him, his mum, complete with long hair, and the dress that had allowed her legs to burn. Then, another figure: a man, taller than them both, with short hair. He showed them and repeated the word, *'Far! Far!'*

'Jesus,' Pop said. Looking at the boy. 'Yer dad?'

The boy indicated how this man had left him and his mum at the car, and walked into the desert, further away from them, to the west.

Nan said, 'He's still out there?'

The boy seemed to sense they understood. He pointed to the front door.

'I'm sure he would've found someone,' Nan said.

But Pop indicated the drawing, and how the man was walking towards the sun, and said, 'Right, come on.'

Things moved quickly. I'm sure Pop had no desire to return to the desert, but he guessed this man had no water either. He went out to the Dodge, spent a few minutes filling the tank, and then fetching two more jerry cans. Water, food Nan quickly wrapped in wax paper, then he knelt down, kissed my dad and said, 'Look after your mum.'

The boy got in beside Pop, and they drove off. Through the gates, out into the desert. For three hours, the stock agent reckoned. Before Pop's fuel pump gave up, and they got out and started heading back, but never made it.

Sitting here still, in my box of bones. Once, Mum suggested we should burn them on a fire. If you threw on a roo it would burn hot with all the guts and fat and the bones would turn to powder, and this little boy (whose name, we found out later, was Geir) would mix with Pop, and we could sprinkle their ashes. Because they'd died together, hadn't they? Walked for two days, and the agent said he'd found Pop a few yards from the road where he'd tried to dig a trench for them to rest in, but hadn't got far before he'd stopped. The agent said there were footprints, going around in circles, but by then the sand had almost reclaimed them. Anyway, when the agent had picked up the bones (the ones he'd found), he'd brought them back in a gunny sack, and Dad had built the box, and put them in, together. And there they'd stayed. Even after the family had written and asked for them. They'd stayed. As with the mum (Agot) who Nan had buried.

All of this, barely mentioned when I was a kid. Perhaps Mum and Dad didn't like to discuss disasters, as our life turned into one. The weeds. The way the door on the shed banged at night because no one could be bothered fixing it.

Toucan darkness

Rochus sets off in the late afternoon. The air is crisp, nearly frozen, and Mama says there'll be snow tonight. He doesn't mind. He has two friends living on his street (Stefan and Peter – and his little brother, Wulf), and they often go up to the hills and toboggan in the snow, and sometimes skate on the Oder, if the mayor, or his assistant, or whoever it is, says the ice is thick enough. But that'll be tomorrow. For now, he has to make his delivery.

He crosses the Palaisplatz, climbs the few steps outside the State Theatre and reads about a new production of *Faust*. This interests him, as his uncle, Georg, to whom he's meant to be taking the food in the aluminium pot, often reads him snatches of Goethe, Thomas Mann, other books in his small room above the stables. Rochus admires the photographs of previous productions and decides to ask his mother if she'll take him. It's the least she can do, considering his daily job in sun, rain, snow, carrying the same pot, rushing (so the food won't go cold) across Breslau to the farm on the edge of town.

Rochus continues along Friedrichstrasse, Luisenplatz, and starts up the hill to the south, to where the farms begin, the sheep, the cows, the nice smells of bulbs and wet hay, where he and Peter and Wulf sometimes climb trees or steal eggs or swim in the lake.

He arrives at the farm, passes the farmer (to whom he never speaks) follows the old lane along the fence to the stables. Then he climbs the rickety steps, avoiding the fifth tread (he counts) that has collapsed beneath his weight before. He knocks on the door and says, 'Uncle Georg?' He hears movement inside. 'Uncle?' Then the door opens and his uncle smiles at him, rubs his hair (messing the part his Mama has just made) and says, 'You shouldn't have come. I've got plenty from yesterday.'

None of this matters, because Mama insists he comes every day, to check on his uncle (her brother), to see that he's coping. Rochus can do this very quickly. Like today. Georg, with his week's whiskers, bloodshot eyes, pale face (he never comes out of his room – this is the farmer's condition, that he doesn't become a nuisance around the farm), his wiry fingers, his hands, shaking, as he reaches for his pot, takes off the lid, sniffs it and says, 'Stew again?'

Rochus shrugs. 'I have to eat it, too.'

'Of course.' Smiling, messing his hair again, inviting him into his room.

Seven out of ten. Most days he's five, six, seven, sometimes he'll have a good day, eight or nine, and very occasionally, a great day – ten. Then his eyes are clear, his face shaved, his hands still, and he'll talk (according to Mama) like he used to, all calm and confident, smart, teaching at the gymnasium, getting about with Rachel, although she's 'long gone' (according to Mama).

The room is dark, musty, and the floor, as usual, is covered with his uncle's filthy clothes. It will be his job to gather them in the sack, take them home for Mama to wash. There's hardly any light coming in, so Rochus pulls back the blinds, and his uncle closes them, sits on the bed and says, 'How's school?'

'No different.' Sitting on a rickety chair.

'It used to be a good school.' He uses his fingers to start eating the stew. Rochus tells him he shouldn't, finds a fork in the sink full of dirty dishes and old food, gives it to him, holds it in his hand, shows him, again, how to eat properly. Georg tries his best eating this way, but his hands are shaking too much and he drops the fork and uses his fingers again. Rochus knows there's no point trying to stop him. He says, 'Herr Reichert keeps going on about Hitler.'

Georg says, 'Yes.' Loading carrots and meat, peas and gravy into his mouth, spilling down his chin, onto his clothes, trying to clean himself. Rochus fetches a towel from the small bathroom (a basin in the corner) and wipes him. This is the easiest way. His uncle seems unaware of the smell from all of this old food, piss, the shitty toilet, the horses and their manure.

'Bad, could be bad,' his uncle says.

'Sorry?'

'Hitler. He comes from the hills, charging down, you know what I mean?' Laughing to himself. 'Like a unicorn, with a horn, you know those, they've taught you about those? Not real, of course, but they go charging about and catch animals on the … whatever it is. That's what they do. They ever teach you about that? Does Reichert teach you about that? He told me he'd take care of me. He did. He certainly did. That's what they should be teaching. Unicorns. Cos Hitler, he's a unicorn, charging down from the hills, you know?'

'Hitler's not a unicorn.'

'Might be. One day. You wait and see. You keep away from him, got it? He doesn't like books like this.' Picking up a volume by someone called Marx, waving it about, then throwing it on the pile of books on the pile of clothes on the pile of rubbish Rochus can't make out.

'Papa says we shouldn't talk about him.'

'Down from the hills …' Tipping the stew straight into his

mouth, more going down his front, Rochus wiping it, Georg pushing him away.

Rochus isn't sure how his uncle has ended up in the room above the stables, on the farm on the edge of town. Whenever he asks Mama, she says, 'It's a long story.' And he says, 'So?' And she says, 'Not today, please, Rochus.' Waving him away. He knows there's no point pursuing it when she gets like this. But somehow (he's worked out) his uncle has lost his job (he suspects this has to do with the red flag hanging in his room, the portraits of bearded men, the types of books he reads, the stuff he tried to teach his students), never found another job, lived with them for a while, lived with other friends, then started 'straying' (Mama's words), wandering town, getting arrested, having to front up to doctors. In fact, this still happens. Only the week before, a neighbour knocking on their door at three am, saying, 'Gert, your brother, on Gartenstrasse.' They found him wandering in his underwear, reciting poetry from the rotunda, blowing on his hands, singing to the birds, asleep on the maypole. They brought him home, put him to bed, fed him and, when he was better, returned him to his room above the stables.

Rochus feels bad for his uncle. 'Mama says she can send more coffee.'

'Good.' Wiping his face, placing the pot on the crowded table beside his bed.

'Coffee is hard to get a hold of.'

'Of course. It's a long way from Brazil, isn't it, Rochus? Toucans and jungles, and they have to be removed if you want to grow coffee, so maybe it'd be best if none of us did, and the toucans, there'd be millions of toucans, wouldn't there, Rochus, covering the sky, and it'd be so dark you couldn't see the sun, and we'd all live in darkness, toucan darkness.' Smiling. Reaching out and touching his nephew's knee, because he (Rochus guesses) still loves him, despite no longer being able to show it. 'South America, equatorial, tropical, of course, above latitude seventy three minutes, fifteen degrees, degrees ...' Repeating the word again and again, until Rochus says, 'Have you had enough to eat?'

'Yes. Thank you.' More, for the opportunity to dampen his brain, his mouth, every moment of every day. 'Say thanks to Mama, my sister, what a sister, Rochus, the best person you'd ever meet, you'll ever meet, making pinnies with Mama, and hanging them about.' Looking at the little bit of light coming through the blinds. 'The best sister, sister – you have one – no, of course, you don't ... a brother, no, maybe it's just you, is it just you, Rochus?'

'No, remember, Franz?'

Thinking. 'Yes, nine, ten, is he?'

'Three.'

'No, he's not? Three? I remember a boy, an older one, like you, but he wasn't you, was he, Rochus?'

'No, he's three, just a little kid. You know, you see him all the time.'

In the little bit of light, trying to remember. But something else has happened, Rochus guesses. He wants to know, so he can do something about it, fix his uncle, make him into the excellent teacher (Mama says) he used to be. There must be a way, he thinks. 'When I come back on Saturday I can take you for a walk again, Uncle.'

'That'll be good. The south, with the better views, the mountains, you could look at those forever, couldn't you, Philip?'

'Rochus.'

'Rochus?' Staring at him. 'Rochus.' Then putting his head in his hands, like something was going, or gone. 'A view of the mountains can fix anything.'

'Can it?' Rochus asks.

'Anything, Rochus Mohr. Like me. A Mohr. I bet you're glad.'

'Of course.'

Rochus feels bad. He rubs his uncle's arm, and wants so much to fix him. 'I'll be back on Saturday,' he says. 'We can go as far as you like.'

'Good.' Settling, letting his head drop, his breathing slow. 'Good, Rochus.' Taking another look at him. 'The glaciers, of course, carved the valley, the valley, deep, over millions of years, millions, billions they teach you about that? Do they? They should. Some of the Lutherans won't, because they think God did it all in six days, but he didn't, he didn't, he didn't even exist, Rochus. Believe me, if he did ... if he answered prayers. Does he, Rochus? Does he answer prayers?'

'Mama says so.'

'She would.' Thinking. 'You're going, are you?'

'It's getting dark.'

'I'd like you to stay, you could, I could make you some food' – and he half-stands, and clears his small table – 'but then, what's there I could make?' Shaking his head. 'Maybe it's best you go home. But you'll come back, won't you, Rochus?'

'Saturday, Uncle.'

'Good, I look forward to that. Saturday. The highest we can, into the clouds maybe, and you could bring your friend.'

'Peter?'

'Yes. The Maiers. They're an old Breslau family. Old, back and back and back, been going, selling something, beans, is it, for years, selling them for years from the same shop in Eisenstrasse, is that still there, Rochus? I went to see the other day, but your Mama brought me home, so I wasn't sure ...'

'I've got to go.'

'Good.' He puts the lid on the pot, and Rochus gathers his clothes and leaves.

Rochus wakes on Saturday morning, determined. He looks out of the window to make sure it's a good day. Indeed. With the sun already blaring, a light breeze, and the same birds flying about the crowded roofs of his neighbourhood.

He wastes no time. He sits up, pulls on his pants, his shirt, his hiking boots, runs to the bathroom and brushes his teeth, returns for his pocket knife, his barley sugar, his keys. 'Mama,' he calls, 'remember, I promised Uncle Georg.'

There's quiet for a few moments.

'Mama?'

Then she and Papa are standing in the doorway. This is unusual. They never agree, or act, on anything. Mama says, 'Not today.'

'I promised Uncle.'

She comes over to his bed, sits and pats the sheets so he might sit, too. Then she says, 'Uncle's gone.'

'Where?'

Papa is still in the doorway, and says, 'It was his choice, Rochus.'

Rochus takes it all in quickly, as quickly as the speed his uncle uses to understand the new world, the Hitler world, the world of unicorns and toucans. 'What do you mean?' he asks his father.

'What I said. His choice. We did what we could.'

Like that. Like it'd all been finished, summarised, written up, filed, forgotten. He looks at Mama and says, 'What?'

'The dam. The farmer found him this morning.'

Rochus can feel his hands shaking, his eyes welling, and words slushing around his head. 'But we're going hiking?'

'Not any more,' his father says, and turns and walks off.

Rochus says to Mama, 'Maybe it's someone else?'

'The farmer sent his son to tell us.'

'But it can't be, we'd arranged …'

They sit in silence, the breeze coming in the window, the voices of kids playing on the freshly surfaced street, like everything is as normal, as happy as it ever has been.

The holotype

This only happened a decade or so after the lighthouse was built. The passage through Investigator Strait, from west to east, under the bottom of the boat of New Holland, this deep blue ripple of life and love and possibilities for the hundreds of thousands who passed on their way to Adelaide, Melbourne, Hobart. Problem being, the shoals. Troubridge Shoals, sand shifting and settling in the anti-clockwise ocean. By the time Job Caswell and Hedley Davis rowed their boat across the warm, gull-flecked sea, thirty-three ships had already been wrecked, some salvaged by the Edithburgh locals, others left to rot. The old colonists said there had been more (the government had called a commission, but the members had never reported). All the fault of Matthew Flinders, rushing past, forgetting to show the shoals. Even then, they were so changeable that maps could hardly be relied upon.

The high point of the shoals was Troubridge Island, an acre of marram- and mallow-covered sand, not far from where Gulliver had crawled ashore. And the highpoint of this, Troubridge Island lighthouse, made in England, shipped to South Australia, its three segments erected on the shifting island in 1855. There'd been a ceremony on the mainland (the island too small for the dignitaries), the cost invoked (£9396), the weight (340 tonnes), the lantern described (a new holophotal reflector), the oil bath, the weights and chains that would need to be wound every four hours during the night to keep the light turning. Sherry was drunk and Cornish pasties, minus meat, consumed in the century heat as flies descended and nipped arms, tried for the little bit of moisture in people's eyes. Hedley Davis had been there with his wife, Margaret, and neighbours, the mayor, dozens of children running about, marvelling at the new structure on the horizon. As the currents lifted the sand, undermining the foundations of the candy-striped tower.

Less than a decade before. And now Hedley, a local farmer with a few acres of wheat, a few sheep, a few thirsty cattle, was rowing the small boat towards Troubridge Island. Over the ridgeback shoals, with their daily muscling, their hide, their skin, like a rhino (Hedley would tell his son, when they went fishing). At times, one could step out, stand up to his or her hips, feel the current on thighs, the gap between leg and scrotum, the belly. Hedley did this; his son did, his feet sinking into the sand. But not today. Today Hedley was rowing (for a pound) Job Caswell to the island. Hedley was doing the work as Caswell watched, mumbled a few words now and then, examined the seascape, the shoals, with his binoculars. Caswell had supplied the shotgun, now sitting between them. He'd explained what it was for (the previous evening, at the front bar of the Royal Hotel). He'd said how he was a scientist, and made his money, filled his days, his years, his life, providing holotypes for the British Museum. But he'd explained how he was no great shooter, like Mr Darwin's, and relied on others to do that work for him. Lately (the last three years), he'd had a helper, Lewis, but he'd selfishly died and left him at a loose end. So now you, Mr Davis, have been recommended. Hedley (finishing the one drink his wife allowed him every week) had said, 'I'm no better than a hundred others, Mr Caswell.'

'That's not what I hear.' Producing the pound note, flattening it on the bar and saying, 'One day's work.'

Hedley had picked it up, finished some quick sums in his head – how many pints it might buy, a spade, bread, even, for the wife and boy. He'd said, 'A day?'

'That's all.' Explaining how he needed to be rowed out to this island where, from all reports, there was a good number of sea birds, and plenty (this time of year) of black-faced cormorants (*Phalacrocorax fuscescens*). He didn't say what the museum paid him for a decent specimen, but he did say, 'And terns … there should be some around?'

'I think so, sir.'

'The Caspian tern. You know it?'

'No, sir, but there are plenty of birds, day and night, and Blake, the keeper, says it's just as well he works at night, because he certainly couldn't sleep.'

So the pound was accepted, handshake shared, and Hedley Davis offered for Mr Caswell to come and stay the night in his hut, but Mr Caswell explained he'd already settled into the Royal's one remaining room.

Back in the boat, Hedley said, 'You do a lot of this?'

But Job didn't seem to hear him. 'This Mr Blake …?'

'Yes, sir.'

'You know him?'

'He's alone, now, sir.'

'You needn't call me sir.'

'His wife came with him, but only lasted a month. She said they should return to Adelaide, but he wouldn't go.'

Hedley Davis rowed. The island, the lighthouse getting bigger, gaining definition. He could make out the patches of boxthorn and sea rocket. He still wasn't sure about this Caswell character. Why come all the way to Troubridge Island for a bird? 'You stuff them, sir?'

'*I* don't.' He was caught up in the view.

'And then what?'

'They're sketched, described, mounted.' And looking at his rower. 'So people might understand what's happening in this country. What it looks like.'

This made sense to Hedley. Australia was nothing like the old country, and how would people know, except for these scientists with their pound notes and guns.

'You're a good shot?' Job asked, looking at his rower again.

'Passable.'

But then returning his gaze to the island, the silver gulls descending and lifting, coming and going like the current.

'Is there a demand?' Hedley asked, stopping for a moment, spitting in his hands, rubbing them on his pants, then continuing.

'Of course.'

Hedley wondered if this work mightn't be easier than farming. He *was* a good shot. His father had taught him well, taking him to Bool Lagoon as a child, training him to be patient, to scan the whole landscape at one time, to hold his gun steady and only ever *squeeze* the trigger.

Hedley said, 'Where are you headed next?'

'West.' Half-smiling at his new friend. 'Why do you ask?'

'You'll need someone?'

'You have a farm.'

Hedley didn't reply. Yes, he had a farm, but his few sheep could get along, his crop wasn't worth harvesting. 'How far west?'

'We'll see.' Returning to his binoculars. 'I can't see anyone.'

'Can you see his boat?'

'No.'

'He might've gone to Edithburgh for supplies.'

This time, Job Caswell had a full smile. 'Good.'

'Sir?'

'Why are there two cottages?'

Hedley seemed to be struggling. He sat up, pushed out his belly, pushed in his back and said, 'That didn't work out.' But continued rowing. 'The first keeper lived in the lighthouse. The tide was at the door. When the sands shifted they built a cottage, but it was washed away. Then another, and Blake moved in. Then they employed another keeper, and he had a wife and two girls, and him and Blake didn't get along, so they built another cottage, but then this second fella, this Quaid, left anyway, and they haven't been able to replace him.'

Caswell didn't seem concerned. 'For supplies, you reckon?'

Hedley strained to see the beach, the many beaches, the all beach of the small island. 'Looks like we're alone.'

As they came closer, Job said, 'Penguins, too?'

'Plenty of penguins. You after some, sir?'

'No, I've collected several. But there, see, cormorants.' Indicating.

'Yes, sir.'

Job studied them, reached for his shotgun, opened the breech and checked for shells. 'I'll take a male and female if I may?' As though he were asking Hedley for permission.

There was a lot Hedley Davis didn't know about Job Caswell. For a start, that he was born in Edinburgh, and grew up with an angry father, a banker, a man who'd never seen the point of having children, who'd compromised to keep his wife happy. So Job was only ever in the background. He'd worked out, and accepted, his ghost status early on. When the family had toured the Old Town under the Royal Mile, the musty earth-hacked rooms, pens and passageways where hundreds had lived like moles, Job had heard his father say things like, 'Good place to keep children.' Smiling, laughing. Although it was no joke.

So Job had kept to his small, sparse, rug-less room overlooking Dalry Cemetery in Edinburgh West. His Saturday morning walks between the gravestones, the stories of taken too soon and in God's arms. That's what he learned about life. That people were born, fed porridge, sent to hospital, then deposited in their burying ground. Some, the stones explained, only lasted long enough to taste the fog and shadows. Others, seventy, eighty years. He couldn't see how anyone could last this long (or would want to), ears against walls, smelling the damp mortar, listening to shouting fathers. Better to line up for death, to join the symmetry of an awkward eternity, add to the pattern that repeated for no purpose, and little effect. Then across the road, up to his room, and a similar collection – this time, matchboxes from around the Empire, tin soldiers, a collection of advertisements he kept in scrap books, a box of cigarettes smoked to various lengths.

Hedley pulled the boat up onto the sand. He stepped in and retrieved the shotgun, and stood waiting for Job, who said, 'It's not much of a place.'

'Full of ghosts, they reckon.'

Hedley just pointed to a few wrecks, persisting on the shoals around them. 'And a boy called Luke (Blake reckons), who lives at the top.'

They both looked up to the lamp. No boy, but Job waited with recognition. The view from his window, the shipwrecks of Edinburgh West. 'He died?' he asked Hedley.

'Blake kept him alive for a few hours, then buried him. The *Adella*, see, out there.' Looking at an iron hull waiting patiently in the offing.

They circumnavigated the island by foot. Once around,

thirty minutes, perhaps. Job said there was no rush, he wanted to be sure of what was worth collecting and lugging back to Edithburgh, to Adelaide, to package and return to England. That all cost money, and believe it or not, he told Hedley, I don't make that much. The terns, the Pacific gulls, the little penguins. Plenty, as promised. But Job didn't seem excited. Someone had used a rope to make a swing, anchored from a rusted frame. Hedley said, 'Let me know what it is you want.'

They returned to the lighthouse, went in, but there was no sign of Blake. To the cottage, and the cheese left out, the bed unmade, the smells of a man who had no one to care for, and cared for no one, who only ever bothered washing when he had to, who hadn't cleaned his toilet, ever, who scraped the mould from his bread before eating it. Hedley and Job sat down and drank warm, sandy water. There was a fob watch, taken apart, and a picture that had been coloured in with five or six crayons. They spent a few minutes talking about firearms, and Job explained how, after years of trial and error, he'd settled on a 16-gauge, 28 inch gun. There was nothing worse than a mutilated bird. But then the conversation had flagged, and Job studied the four white-washed walls and said, 'This place would be enough to send a man mad.'

Hedley thought he was joking, but as the narrator of this true story, I can tell you, he wasn't. Living alone is enough to send anyone mad. A small, cold Scottish bedroom, where you ended up passing a needle through your finger to see if you could get to the other side, to see if you could bear the pain. Because there was never anyone at the door (except Missi, the maid), and you weren't allowed to go downstairs during the day, especially on the weekend when father was home.

'I'd be happy to have you along,' Job said to Hedley.

'The west?'

'What would your wife say?'

'She'd agree, sir.'

'Call me Job.' The same half-smile as when he saw a specimen that would do, nicely.

So Job grows up, is sent to boarding school, runs away and jumps a ship out of Glasgow. He arrives in Port Adelaide and, straight away, sets off for the distant country, the red soil, mallee, the skeletal trees shedding branches through hot summers, the waterless creeks and birdless skies. He takes a wife and finds, after all, he's just as angry as his father. Or more correctly, the land *makes* him angry. The way there's no water for months, years, and his animals die, and he finds out what it's like to be poor, to live in the Old Town of the New Country, endless land but the worst sort of claustrophobia. Like you can ride forever, but go nowhere except the same small room with its mutton cooking, its flies, its heat, its wife, telling you what a failure you are, after all.

'Come on then,' Job said.

Out, through the nitre bush, towards the low part of the island, the water lapping at their feet, the cormorants wading offshore. Job handed Hedley the shotgun, indicated a bird, and said, 'That one looks the goods.'

Hedley lined it up, then said, 'We should get closer.'

But Job had seen something more interesting. He turned towards the box thorn on what passed as a hill and said, 'Is it really?'

Hedley put down his gun, and looked.

Because, reader, it was the same gun Job had bought upon his arrival in Port Adelaide. He'd had this idea from the beginning. He'd thought, each animal is a tin type, and might be harvested, lined up, marched as an army across the bedroom floor. He'd thought, I could collect the night parrot, and be paid well. He'd even gone on an expedition with a Mr Calvert, roamed the state for months, shot mammals, birds, anything that moved, really. Mr Calvert had taken some, but left piles of corpses to rot. Which made Job Caswell, himself, a holotype. Although not now. He couldn't bear to shoot anything now.

'Who is he?' Job asked Hedley.

Both men walked the ten or fifteen yards, across sand that moved as they moved, through hairy spinifex that left burrs on their pants and socks.

I should explain why Job Caswell employed a shooter. It was his twenty-first birthday. He and his wife were sitting on what passed as a porch, watching for the nothing-in-particular that made up their life. There was an argument about returning to town, Job saying they hadn't given it long enough, his wife saying more than enough! – going in and starting to pack her bag. Enraged, Job had picked up his shotgun and followed her.

Her name was Kate, and she was his first holotype, his first perfect specimen, dragged outside into the tea-tree, laid in a shallow grave and covered.

'What's your name?' Job asked the six- or seven-year-old boy. No reply.

A small, bony boy. A black boy. A swinging boy. A boy with coloured fingers and jam around his mouth. It was ridiculous to think that Blake, or any man, could live without companionship.

The boy, who'd been watching them, who'd been squatting, sat in the grass and managed, 'He's gone for bread.'

Job looked to Hedley for an explanation, but he couldn't provide one.

Job turned a complete revolution, studied the island, the sea, the acres of emptiness that had so often marked his feeling, his need, his desire to describe things, to have them understood, pinned to a board, copperplate Latin in the Linnaean mode. 'Imagine what I could get for him,' he said to Hedley.

'Sir?' Confused.

Job had then burned his cottage, and scattered it as best he could. This is the story he never told because, simply, he'd got away with it. Indeed, it wasn't hard to get away with anything. The specimens were salted, packed and dispatched.

But then Hedley realised what his new boss meant. 'But he's ...'

The boy was pissing himself. Job went to take the gun from Hedley, but he wouldn't give it up. Job explained that it belonged to him, and as they argued, the boy ran away, across the island, into the lighthouse.

'If you want the work?' Job said, calmly.

So slowly, Hedley yielded. He sat in the damp grass as Job went up to the lighthouse. Through such means of diligence, observation and science, he would create an understanding of this continent, the one he'd adopted, and which had adopted him. A new history of Australia, with plentiful illustrations and a handsome frontispiece. To help him understand, at last, the view from his Edinburgh bedroom.

The tree, the sky, the heaven

Jochen runs from his house, jumps the fallen fence and stands, looking around, trying to decide. He glances back at the house, curious to think if it's happened yet, if Papa has eaten his lunch. Maybe he'll hear something? Choking? His mother's screams? He listens, but all he can hear is the sway, the creak of trees, the brushing of one leaf against another, multiplied a million, a billion times. He can hear St Martin's bell, telling him it's lunch time, telling him his father will be sitting down to rabbit stew and boiled potatoes.

Jochen Lemmer is eleven years old, but tall, and his head hangs from a long neck. He's recently joined the Jungvolk and enjoys hikes, sport, chariot races, the getting out and doing things (although not so much the lectures). He likes to hang back, and offer an opinion (when it's asked for), but he doesn't like the idea of leading. Better to watch, to think, to take your time, to pace yourself, to plan. He likes studying history, and science, and tries at maths, although his answers are rarely the same as those in the back of the text book.

Jochen wonders whether he should run down the lane, towards the last of the hops, but decides it won't change a thing. It'll soon become clear to everyone. So he'll have to wait and deal with the consequences. It's important to put everything out of his head. He decides, sees the oak tree, the steps his father has nailed on (and thinks, if he's done this, then he's not terrible, is he?) and knows this is the best place to wait. So he runs another hundred yards, climbs the few steps, into the foliage, the dark, cool world he loves the most. He sits on the small platform (his father has put there, for him) and waits. He crosses his legs, watches the house, listens, but there's no sound, no movement, no dramas. Just a few birds sitting around him, curious, wondering (he supposes) if he's brought seed.

Nothing to do but wait. Maybe no one will guess. He has, after all, replaced the packet of Rodine ('Rapid Rat Removal') in its spot in the cellar. He's slipped it behind the disinfectant, the teak oil, the other bottles labelled POISON and CAUTION. In fact, he's done a good job. He's gone (that morning, after finally deciding) down to the cellar, searched for the Rodine, emptied some into a paper bag. He's read the instructions and worked out that one grain can kill a rat. Therefore, four grains for four rats, times a hundred for his father's bulk, equals forty grains. But then he's had to estimate. Three and half spoonfuls, and half to make sure. He's done the maths on the back of an envelope with a blunt pencil. He's double-checked his figures. He doesn't want to do a shit-faced job (Papa always telling him he's a shit-faced worker).

After a while (he checks) his heart rate drops, moisture returns to his mouth and the light breeze through the branches dries his forehead, his face, his clothes. He listens. Papa should be eating by now. He always comes in from feeding the pigs, washes his hands, sits waiting for Mama to put food in front of him; he moves the plate about, examines it, says something like, 'It's full of fat,' or 'This is the tenth day in a row,' before eating it. And when he, Jochen, joins them, Papa says, 'What have you been up to this morning?' He says (for example), 'I went into town to visit Peter,' and Papa replies, 'Didn't you have school work?'

'I finished it.'

'You always say that, then you come home with bad grades. Why don't you finish it *properly*?'

Like this. It might be about chores, or spending time with his sister, mucking out the cattle pens, or maybe the time he wastes sitting up his tree reading nonsense.

He remembers. His favourite, his most valuable comic (*Sheena, Queen of the Jungle*), rolled up, slipped in a knothole. It's a great spot, because the hole is hidden by the branch, and Sheena can't get wet. It's in far enough that birds, or rodents, can't get to it. He pulls it out, flattens it, checks the house, then admires the cover: Sheena, in a skimpy leopard skin dress that shows her legs, and most of her breasts, clutching a dagger (like Peter's), looking at the reader as two hungry panthers close in around her. Sheena ('Wild Beauty of the Congo') isn't scared of anything or anyone. If she lived near Breslau she wouldn't be scared of Papa. She'd go in there now and gut him, top to bottom, with her dagger. Her long, golden locks. Her perfect teeth. The suggestion of a nipple (the image enough to allow him to strip her, hold her, run his hands over her skin).

He checks the house again. Surely Papa would've started eating by now? Put on his bib, shovelled rabbit into his mouth, ground it with his loud, clunkety jaw, got angry about something. If he did something wrong, his Papa would drag him out to the pigs, throw him in the pen, stand laughing. Once he even turned the hose on him. But it was worse for Mama. Papa would take her into their room, and he'd have to take Annie outside, help her up the tree, read to her. Another one of the comics his uncle had sent from England (the ones, that is, that had got past Papa, always shredding them, saying how ridiculous it was, and England, of all places!).

But today is different. Annie is off on a hike with her league of girls. Jochen saw the date on the calendar weeks before and planned it all in his head. Rodine day. 'R' day. A bit like Sheena day, swinging from a vine, landing, kicking a carpet of skulls and saying, 'Come and eat me, lion.' Thing being (Jochen told his sister, as they sat up the tree), Sheena has the ability to transform into any animal with whom she makes eye contact. Annie saying, 'How can a person become an animal?'

'Sheena can. That's how she's survived. She would've been eaten years ago if she was just a person. She's had to adapt.'

'Into a tiger?'

'If need be.'

He checks the house again. Maybe Papa's eaten the stew, and maybe he's coughed up blood, choked, and Mama's left him on the floor, dead as a Saturday pig, strung up ready for skinning. Or maybe he hasn't started yet? Maybe he's still washing his hands or checking a bill or reading the newspaper, and maybe there's still time to go down and stop what he's begun, what (he knows, somehow, they'll find out) he'll have to pay for, the rest of his life.

To stop these thoughts, he returns to Sheena. 'The Doom of the Elephant Drum' isn't as simple as it seems. In English, of course, so he's had to translate it, cell by cell, using a small English-German dictionary, and the few dozen words he's picked up off the radio, or from Herr Philip, his teacher. Cell 1, for example: 'SHEENA LOVES ANIMALS OF JUNGLE, CARES FOR THEM, BECOMES THEM, EVEN IN THE RHINOCERUS'. Some words aren't in his dictionary, so he's had to rely on images. Either way, this German Sheena is what he uses when he reads to his sister, up their tree, waiting for Papa's fury to subside.

It had to be done quickly. The bowl in his father's spot, saying to his Mama, 'Papa wants you in the shed.' She'd gone out, he'd opened his bag, emptied the grains, spent a few seconds stirring them until they dissolved. Rinsing the spoon in the sink, putting it in his pocket with the screwed up bag. As he thought of them now, found another hole and forced them in, then plugged this with leaves, sticks, and spread sap over the lot. No one would think to look up here.

Still nothing. Surely he's eaten by now. Surely he's dead? Because he deserved to be dead. He was Breslau's, Germany's, the world's King of Humiliation. The worst example, and the one that had made him decide, was the previous Monday. He'd snuck Sheena inside, gone to bed, laid between clean sheets admiring her. This had made him happy, hot, like the pigs in heat, the cows when the bull was hired for the day. One thing leading to another, and there he was, ten minutes later, standing in the shower. His father had come in, seen him, shouted at him, dragged him naked out into the rain and said, 'Think about what you do in my house.' He'd picked him up, thrown him in the cow's trough, and held him down. Then he'd gone back inside. Mama looking out at him. His sister, wondering. He'd run into the shed, covered himself with hay and waited, shivering, before Mama came out with dry clothes.

Some things were unforgivable. They couldn't be undone, unseen, or even apologised for. Sometimes (like Sheena) if a wild animal was after you, you just had to change into a stronger, meaner, nastier version of yourself. It was the law of the jungle, the survival of the fittest. Like Hitler said, 'No mercy for the weak.'

He checks again, becomes anxious again, and stills himself by translating another cell: 'WHAT IS IT YOU COMPLAIN ABOUT, HERR JONES, TROPHY HUNTERS DESERVE THE

SAME AS THEIR TROPHIES. SHALL I RETURN [?*zuruck perhaps, go back, something* ...] YOU TO OXFORD IN A BOX WITH YOUR ELEPHANT TUSKS?'

He's unhappy with this, and scribbles it out. He knows it doesn't have the sense, the feel, the bubblegum wit and style of American English. He's asked his great uncle (who lived in America for six years) and he's helped with a few phrases, but it's a long comic with thousands of words and he fears he'll never get to the end. Especially if ... unless he can take his comics with him.

What will it be like? Will he have his own room? Will the boys be reasonable, like him? Will they be happy to sit around at night, helping him translate Sheena or Superman (due next month)? Or will it be terrible? Things that happen when no one's watching? Regardless, Mama and Annie will be safe, able to get on with living at last.

This can't be right. His father would have eaten by now. So, with trembling hands, he rolls up his comic, his translation, and returns it to its hole. He climbs down and walks towards the house, listening. He hears coughing, and stops. A loud, meaty cough. Then his father emerges from the front door and says, 'Your mother was calling for you.' He coughs again, rests against the door frame, says, 'That was off,' and turns and vomits into the garden.

Mama comes out and says, 'What's wrong?'

'What was in that stew?' Wiping food from his mouth.

'It'd only just been killed.'

His father stops, says, 'You been up your tree again?'

He shrugs.

'I need you to chop some wood.' Indicating the pile.

Papa walks away, spitting the last of the stew from his mouth, sits on the tractor, starts it, drives down the lane towards the hops. Mama steps towards him, hands him the envelope with the figures and says, 'He'd eaten half before I realised.'

He examines the writing. 'Where …?'

'You left it beside the stew.'

'I didn't actually … I thought about it, but I didn't.'

She shakes her head and says, 'You were never good at maths. Forty grains was never enough.'

He curses himself. Not so much for the maths, as the quality of the idea. He can see it now, from above, from the tree, the sky, the heaven he can reach up and touch with his hand (nearly).

Mama says, 'He mightn't be much of a father, but he's the only one you've got.'

Mrs Meiners has gone to get chalk

Mrs Meiners' class is all seven- and eight-year-olds. Enrolments are down, three classes have become two, and even then, she only has fourteen students. This morning the class is even smaller. The Baker twins are off with a flute lesson, two boys (the trouble-makers, 'Smith and Wesson') are at a sports carnival in Philadelphia, and Blake Clare has the flu. The remaining nine students are sitting at their tables, working, while Mrs Meiners pops down to the office for supplies. She knows she can trust them (apart from S&W). They're good kids.

Max Rewald is busy with a diorama. The Battle of Waterloo is slowly taking shape on his desk. The red soldiers, the blue soldiers, and little guns he's made from matchsticks. There are plenty of bodies sitting around in the grass, on the hillsides. He wants to make it realistic. He's painted it. Nicely, with red and brown. He says to his friend, Tim, 'It's late for recess.'

Tim says, 'No, it's not.'

'There was no bell.'

'Yes, there was.'

Tim's hungry. It seems like they've been alone for hours. He's busy with his composition. He's writing about the time they went to Walt Disney World and he got sick on the first ride and had to spend most of the day in the cafeteria clutching his guts, and chucking up. 'My sister's keeped returning to see if I was any beter but when I wasnt they just kept going anyway.' He's being careful. He wants to please Mrs Meiners. She's told him he has a very neat hand, beautiful, flowing cursive, and he should keep practising. So he continues, clutching the pencil (too hard), biting his lip. Then he looks up and says, 'Was that the bell?'

'No, it's Mr Reed's walkie-talkie.'

'What's he doing here?'

'He only does the garden on Tuesdays. On Mondays he's the super.'

One desk over, a girl named Kate is colouring an elephant. There's paint all over it, and she smooths it, but it smudges and she shakes her head and says, 'I'm going to start again.' She screws it up, puts it in the bin and gets another blank from Mrs Meiners' desk. Then she sits, selects a green pencil, and starts on the hills.

Her friend, Robin, who's more interested in maths, works through her Speed and Accuracy booklet. Again, the same paint, but she doesn't care, because she just wants to solve the problems. This is important to her. If a sum is left unfinished, then there's something wrong with the balance, the feel, the geometry of the world. She says to Kate, 'Why you doing it again?'

'She said she's going to mark it.'

'Colouring in? She never marks colouring in.'

'Anyone there?' A voice from the hallway. Robin says, 'Mark's brother. He better not come in. Not during second period. He'll get in so much shit.'

'You can't say that.'

'*Shit.*'

Tim and Max try it out. A small chorus of shit, and then Tim tries bugger, but makes sure Mrs Meiners doesn't suddenly come in. That would take some explaining when he got home tonight. Walked in, bag on the couch, his mum messing his hair and asking about his day, kissing him on the top of the head.

Another boy, Sidney, sits in the corner reading a book about a girl who finds a magical frog. He says, 'This is crap,' and searches the Level 6 reader box for another. Kate says, 'You should try Stephen King.'

'Not allowed.'

'I saw this film about a kid and his mum and the dad goes nuts.'

Sidney doesn't care. He just examines his scabby arm, and the blood, and says, 'Do you think I should see the nurse?'

Another boy, Harry, is half-asleep, his head on the desk. Kate tells him he should wake up and finish his maths because Mrs Meiners will be back soon and if he's wasted time she won't be happy.

A light flashing in the hallway. Robin says, 'Do you think he's coming back?'

Max says, 'No, not now he's done. He'll have to find some more kids.'

'Do you think he'll go to Ms Thomas's class? My sister's there.'

'He might.'

'Maybe I should go tell her.'

'You can't.'

'Yeah.' As she deflates. 'I forgot.'

'I can't believe how quickly it happened,' Harry says, finding his spelling book and opening it.

'Everyone's gonna know about us,' Tim says.

'It's not like it's unusual,' Max adds.

'No. Although my mum's going to be really pissed off.'

Then Max checks his watch and says, 'She should be back by now, shouldn't she?'

Tim agrees. He's hungry, and although the clock has fallen from the wall, and lies in pieces on the floor, he guesses it's past time for the bell. 'It didn't ring.'

'Should I check?' Morry, another quiet boy, says.

'She'll give you a detention if she finds out.'

He doesn't care. He takes out his phone and checks the time. 'Yeah, see.' Holding it up. 'The bell should've gone twenty minutes ago.'

They all sit, thinking what to do. No one says anything. Just the nine voices, lost in their own arithmetic, unable to find the correct answer.

Max says, 'Maybe he didn't mean it?'

Tim asks him what, what didn't he mean?

Max just says, 'I was first.'

'I was second,' Kate adds.

'What's it matter who was first?' Morry says.

They hear footsteps, and Kate says, 'He's coming back,' and Morry says, 'It doesn't matter anymore.' And Kate starts crying.

The footsteps get louder, and they clutch the edge of their desks, stand, move into corners, but this time it's a policeman, wearing a bulletproof jacket, carrying the same sort of rifle as him. He says, 'Fuck.' Takes a deep breath, then drops his head, looks away.

'Mrs Meiners has gone to get chalk,' Max says to him.

He doesn't reply. He just unclicks a walkie-talkie from his belt, one like Mr Reed's, and says, 'There are more in here.'

A voice comes back, 'How many?'

He counts. 'Nine.' Then half-collapses against the door jamb, lets his head drop, like a broken doll, and slides down, so he's squatting.

'What's wrong with him?' Max asks the others.

'He's upset about something,' Kate says, standing, trying to decide what to do next.

The budgerigar

I

Tom Joll. Eleven. Standing on the corner of Lily and Foreman Streets, holding an old copy of J.D. Salinger's *Nine Stories*. Jeans, torn about the knees, and a T-shirt his brother, before he died in a motorcycle accident, gave him for his tenth birthday. Now, the top feels strange, creepy, but his mother still makes him wear it, tells him it has years left in it yet. Sometimes, Tom thinks, his mother values money more than people, and all of the things that go between them. A lot has gone between Tom and his brother, Joel. A lot. When Joel died, it was like the world ended and he, Tom, wouldn't possibly be able to continue alone. But he has. Here now, standing on the corner of Lily and Foreman Streets, holding Salinger's book. Worse than that, because when his brother died, Tom was so overcome by *something* (he couldn't say what, still can't) that he ran into Joel's room, opened his window, his bird cage, then waited for his Australian budgerigar to fly out of the room, the house, his life. Almost like, he thought later, the budgerigar was Joel in bird form, a spirit, a ghost that he, Tom, wouldn't allow to haunt him for the rest of his life. Standing at the window, watching it (all green and yellow) sitting on a branch of the oak tree in their front yard, until his mother came in, saw what was happening, slapped him on the back of the head and said, 'Why on earth did you do that?'

So here he is now, on the corner of Lily and Foreman Streets, waiting. A pair of tourists walk by and he steps forward, shows them the book and says, 'I can help … if you like?'

One of them, the man, says, 'Leave it alone, kid. Don't you think he'd like his privacy?'

Tom's used to this, so he just shrugs, turns away, but the young man says, 'Have you ever seen him?'

Tom lights up. 'Yes, plenty of times. He comes into town, walks along here to fetch his mail and buy bread from Mr Franco and milk from … the supermarket, there, see, he always gets milk, he seems to need a lot of milk.'

But this doesn't work, and the man and his wife (or girlfriend, or whoever she is) continue along.

Tom waits. It's all just a matter of waiting. It's money well spent. He charges five dollars, but people usually haggle him down to four, three, a dollar, perhaps, but he doesn't care. It all adds up. He keeps his earnings in a shoe box under his bed and, one day soon, will have the $52 he needs. Then it'll be set right. Then. As he looks up, sees a tall man, a long, box-shaped face, like his head had once been full of groceries but now is just a head. And a nose like a boxer's nose, like it's been hit once too often. He watches this man coming towards him, and he watches how he's staring at him, interested in something. He seems familiar. Why does he seem familiar? As he clutches the book in his sweaty hand (it's ninety-one degrees), rolls it and unrolls it, flattens it, puts it in his pocket, takes it out, but this man is just watching him. He's heard. First, they offer you candy, then they ask if you'd like to come back to their place to see their comics, then they say they've got the very first Superman, then you go with them, then they lock the door behind you and a week later your posters are up around town and people are stopping and chatting and saying, 'Tom Joll, you remember him? Nancy's boy. Joel's brother. He used to stand there, right over there, offering to show people where Jerry lived.'

So he watches this man closely, and the man stops and says, 'You're the boy?'

'What boy?'

'The boy who charges five dollars to show people where Mr Salinger lives?'

Tom still isn't sure. Why would one of those sort of people start off like this, in the middle of Foreman Street, with everyone watching? But he seems familiar. And Tom, this scrawny, underfed, overslapped budgerigar of a boy, tries to think why the man with the box head and the broad shoulders and the long, bony arms is asking him this. So he says, 'Would you like to see?' Because maybe this man is some sort of Salinger reader, or fanatic (people seem obsessed with him – why, he can't say, because he's never read one of his books, despite having a *Nine Stories* and *The Catcher in the Rye* that Joel stole from the school library). People come all the way from New York, California, Germany, England, Australia, even, to catch a glimpse of the writer. Fanatics! So why shouldn't he, Tom Joll, poor, underfed kid, take advantage of the opportunity? Why shouldn't he provide a service? It's not like he's taking them *in* to Mr Salinger's house. Taking them to the front door and knocking and greeting the great man (who, truth tell, he's never seen) and saying, 'Mr Salinger, I'd like to introduce you to Jack Dawes from Australia who's read all of your books and thinks you're the greatest writer in the world.' No. None of this. He's keeping his distance. Thirty yards back. Moving some bushes. Indicating. That's it. How's that disturbing anyone's privacy?

The man (wearing slacks, a jumper, even on a day like this) with the big paddle hands and long fingernails says, 'Okay, then, how much do you want?'

'Five dollars.'

The man stops, thinks, stares at the boy (God, maybe he's an undercover policeman!), then says, 'Fine.' With a wry smile.

Tom holds out his hand for the money but the man says, 'Only after you show me.'

'Half now, half then.'

'I only have a ten … I'll give you ten, if you show me.'

Tom thinks, Okay. Ten. Usually they barter down, not up, but he doesn't care because he can use the money to buy the budgie (that's what they call them in Australia) faster. Then he holds up the book and says to the man, 'Have you read this?' And he says, 'Several times.' Tom says, 'Is he your favourite writer?' The man says, 'Not particularly. He's very ordinary. But since I'm here, I might as well see where he lives.'

II

They set off past the kindergarten, the nursing home, the automotive shop that's recently closed, the fabric shop, a whole lot of shops, across a small playground, up a hill, past St Matthew's, along a narrow and secluded birch-lined path. Tom thinks if this man's a child molester he might act now, but ten dollars is so much money, and without Joel's money (working at the pet shop) there's not so much around to spend now. That's why he's hungry, he wants to tell this man, wearing loafers, some sort of comfortable shoes; he wants to tell him ten dollars is a lot, and thanks, and you'll enjoy seeing this, it's something very few see, because Mr Salinger is very secretive, hides from the community. 'The people in town won't tell you nothing about Mr Salinger.'

'Anything.'

'Sorry?'

'Won't tell you *anything*. And why do you think that is?'

Struggling to get up an incline. Tom offers to help, but the man is more rugged than he seems, moves like a rabbit, like a soldier jumping out of his trench to attack the enemy.

'I think Mr Salinger pays them money to keep quiet. Yes, I think that's true. Why else would they not tell anyone?'

The man stops to pick a leaf from a bay tree, smell it, like he's done this a thousand times before. 'Maybe they just respect his privacy?'

'Could be that, too.' Continuing. 'But what I don't understand is why Mr Salinger hates people so much he wants to live alone and never see no one.'

'*Anyone*. Maybe he's tired of people? How they're always on at him? Want something from him?'

'Maybe.'

Tom is holding back branches so the man can pass through the undergrowth. 'This is where me and Joel used to come to ...' But stops. Why tell him? Who is he? He doesn't deserve to know, hasn't paid enough for him to unload his whole life. So he decides to stop talking, wait for the money, go home and put it in the shoe box. But the man continues: '... used to come to ...?'

Tom says it before he thinks. 'We used to dare each other to see who could climb the highest ...' Gazing around for the tallest tree. 'That one, I think.' Indicating. 'And Joel'd get to the top and look in nests and get eggs and take them home and keep them in cotton, in front of the fire, until they ... then when they hatched he'd take them to work, his job, the pet shop, and they'd sell them. Twenty dollars each, Mr ...?'

'Glass.'

'Mr Glass. Twenty dollars apiece, Mr Glass. And he'd give me five dollars to ...' Slowing. Stopping. Realising he'd given more than ten dollars' worth.

'And where's Joel now?'

Tom stops, peers down a steep incline, realises, if you fell, it'd be unlikely you'd survive. But this is what he did, every day – led people along the path so he could get enough money to replace his brother's budgie. 'He's dead.'

'Your brother?'

Tom nods. Maybe it'd be best to take a few more steps.

'That's a shame, Tom.'

Tom doesn't reply. It's more than a shame. It's shit. It's very shit. Every day it's shit. Every night, lying in bed, talking to no one instead of Joel. Shit.

'Was he sick?' Mr Glass asks.

'No … someone didn't wait for him to … on his motorcycle. A Kawasaki. He reckoned they were best.'

Mr Glass waits for more information, but Tom doesn't want to tell him how Joel was late for work, how he sped off without even waking him, his brother, Tom, and saying goodbye, as he did most mornings, as he should have, if he'd been following the rules of life. No. None of that. Tom woke and his brother was gone and the breeze was blowing in his window and the budgie was chirping and his mother was in the kitchen making pumpkin soup and it was the most ordinary day ever. He, Tom Joll, doesn't want to tell Mr Glass this. 'Come on, we're nearly there.'

Continuing. This is where they had to be careful because the path (as it was) passed through Mr Holland's land and they had to go under a fence, through boggy marsh, another fence, then pass through the open where Mr Holland might be able to see them from his living room, and once, when he and Joel had done this, Mr Holland had come out shouting at them to get off his land.

Mr Glass stops, looks into the sky, wipes his face with a handkerchief, replaces it in his pocket and says, 'It's a lot of work for five dollars, Tom.'

'What else would I be doing?'

'Playing with your friends. Baseball?' Shrugging, almost as though he couldn't imagine what an eleven-year-old would be doing on a day like this.

'I don't care,' Tom says. He stands studying Mr Holland's place, a big, five or six bedroom house on the hill with gardens of red and white camellias that Mrs Holland enters in the Cornish show every year. 'I gotta get $52, anyways, Mr Glass.'

'Why?'

'To buy a budgie.'

'A budgie?' Mr Glass laughs, bends over, places his hands on his knees to support his throaty chuckle, and Tom says, 'What's so funny?'

'A budgie? A little bird? The little green ones?'

'That's it.'

And now Tom can't help but smile.

'You do all of this because you want a budgie?'

'I don't want one but ... I *have* to have one.'

'Why?' From laughter to intrigue, a flash of light from behind the little bit of cloud left in the summer sky.

'I just have to.'

'But why?'

Tom still doesn't want to tell him. Ten dollars only buys so much. Whatever it was between him and Joel should stay between him and Joel.

'If you tell me, I'll give you twenty dollars.' And to make it clear, Mr Glass takes out his wallet, finds a twenty, holds it between his first two fingers, hoping, perhaps, Tom can smell it, taste it, or at least need it more than he can resist it.

'I don't want your money.' And walks on.

III

They pass from Mr Holland's land, and Mr Glass (still holding the twenty) says, 'There must be an easier way to get to Mr Salinger's house?'

Tom shrugs again. There is. But he likes coming this way. He likes the forest and how it's always cooler than the fields; he likes the rustle of leaves; the sound of people harvesting grass with mowers. He likes the country. 'If I had a million dollars I'd buy a farm and be a farmer.' He glances back. He's sure, now, this man isn't one of the men who keep children in their basement. He doesn't look like that. Whatever that is.

'What type of farmer would you be?'

Tom likes this question, can't help himself, says, 'A bird farmer.'

'How can you farm birds?'

'You can. I've seen it on television. You build a big aviary and fill it with girl birds and boy birds of every type and you make millions, well thousands, maybe hundreds of birds. That'd be best. And I'd have all of the birds I want.'

'I have a bird.'

Tom stops and says is it a budgie, though he knows almost no one has an Australian budgerigar, and Mr Glass says it's just an old finch called Seymour, and he's got patches where he's always working at himself. Old and run-down, like me, Tom.

Tom thinks that doesn't sound good at all. A budgie would be better. That would solve everyone's problems.

But it doesn't matter, because they're nearly there. They climb a hill covered in rocks and grass and stray old bushes with rabbit droppings everywhere, and Mr Glass says, 'It's almost impossible to get rid of the rabbits, isn't it, Tom?'

'I guess.' He stops. 'Are you going to give me the twenty?'

'Yes.'

'Can I have it now?'

'*Ah.*' The same smile. 'I still haven't seen Mr Salinger's house.'

So Tom runs up the hill and calls for Mr Glass to keep up and Mr Glass struggles, but manages, because although he's old he's not so old he can't get up a hill. When they're nearly at the top, Tom stops and points at a big, brown wooden house that overlooks the valley and says, 'There it is.'

Mr Glass takes a moment, looks, says, 'Are you sure?'

'Yes.'

'How do you know?'

'Everyone knows ... well, some people know, and Joel knew, and he brought me here to show me and he told me that Mr Salinger is the most famous writer in the world but no one has ever seen him cos he never comes out of his house and he's like a ...' Making a big, fat, full face of a monster. 'Some sort of ghoul.'

'A *ghoul*?' The same laugh. 'So it definitely is Mr Salinger's house?'

'Yes.'

'And if we waited here long enough we'd see him, this Mr Salinger?'

'Yes, definitely.'

'And you'd know what he looks like?'

'No, no one'd know.'

'But you said ...?'

Tom stops to think.

'So why don't we go and see him?' Mr Glass grabs the book

from Tom's pocket, Tom reaches for it, but Mr Glass is too tall. 'Come on.' The old man emerges from the bushes, strides up the hill with long-legged steps Tom hasn't seen so far on the hike. Tom follows him, calling, 'No, stop, we're meant to respect his privacy!'

'Who cares about that? I'm sure he's got a few minutes spare to talk to me about' – checking the book – '*Nine Stories*.'

Tom runs faster, gets in front of Mr Glass and says, 'He gets so angry. Furious. You don't want to!'

Mr Glass waves the twenty dollars in Tom's face.

'He just wants to be left alone. He doesn't like people, for some reason.'

'No?'

'Something happened and now he hates all people and never comes out of his house and if you do this, if you go to his door … you shouldn't, Mr Glass. You should do what he wants. You should …' Out of breath.

But Mr Glass says, 'Nonsense.' He continues up the hill, onto the porch with an old Buddha and a tray of sliced apricots the birds have eaten, approaches the door and calls to Tom, 'Come on, Tom. We've come all this way.'

Tom holds short. It's one thing to look from a distance, but this isn't right. What if something bad has happened to Mr Salinger? What if that's why he wants to be left alone? What if his brother died, too, and he never got over it and misses him and cries for him every day but can't have him so he just sits in his house wishing it hadn't happened like this, wishing he'd said goodbye, wishing the truck had given way, wishing after, he'd not blamed his mum and gone into Joel's room and let the budgie go free.

But there's Mr Glass, on the porch, and he knocks on the

door and says, 'Come on, Tom, I'm sure he's not as horrible as you think. I'm sure he's decent, don't you think, Tom?'

Tom doesn't know. He stands in front of Mr Salinger's house wondering if he's inside and if he can see him and if he's getting angrier and angrier and ready to come out and shout and scream and maybe even hit him or Mr Glass.

'Tom?'

'We oughtn't.'

'Why not?' The same laugh. 'You're a remarkable young man, Tom.' This time, not so much a laugh as a smile, and Tom thinks and thinks and remembers and runs up onto the porch and reclaims the book and looks at the picture on the back cover.

But it doesn't matter. Mr Glass gives him the twenty and says, 'It's not a budgie, I know, but if you want to take Seymour, he's yours.'

Regrets, I've had a few

He picks her up every day after school. Waits in the same spot, the best park, under a pepper tree, which is important on hot days. He welcomes her into the car and asks about her day and she always says something like okay, I guess, or same as every other day, or ssdd (same shit different day), which is something he's taught her, but regrets, as she's only twelve and he's meant to be a good role model. But what's it matter? She giggles a bit, and tells him what mum thinks about his filthy mouth and he says, At least I'm always honest.

Not always.

How?

But she just grins, and he says you weren't meant to see that, and she says loose lips sink ships (another one of his sayings). They drive home and she starts telling him about maths, and how it's way too easy, and aren't schools meant to challenge kids?

What is it? he asks.

Improper fractions … But her attention's caught by the man they always see with the supermarket trolley, pushing it around Gleneagles, going through people's recycling bins and collecting cans and bottles. She says, He can't earn much money that way.

He says, It's not like it's his job.

It might be.

I don't think he's paying rent, power, gas from … cans.

She's taken with an idea. We should ask him why he does it.

It's none of our business.

She seems confused by this. He often tells her she should be engaged, and interested in others, and ask about people's interests and hobbies. So she says, Pull over.

No.

Go on. Tugging on the steering wheel.

Don't do that.

They pass the man with the trolley. She's left wondering, but he doesn't care. At least this man finds a way to fill his days. Some purpose; some meaning. That's all a person needs. So he says, If it keeps him happy.

She doesn't reply. The man's gone. There's plenty more to look at now. Like the bakery that's been closed for years. How hard would it be to reopen it? Up at four, bread, rolls, buns. She's said this before (I could always be a baker) and he's said, You've got a good brain, you should use it.

Whatever keeps you happy?

Within reason.

Soon they're home and his daughter runs in and tells her mum about her day. He waits in the car for a few minutes, studying how the clouds are building, greying in the distance. He searches for zebras or his kids' faces in the nimbus, the threat of rain, the smell of wet wood. An A380 coming in to land. He still can't work out how it stays in the air. Despite the documentaries, it doesn't seem possible. But there it is, he guesses. So much that defies explanation. So he gives up and goes inside and listens to them talking and says to his wife, She forgot her sports uniform again.

His wife asks his daughter, Why did she give you that?

Because I forgot my sports uniform.

I had it on your bed.

She needs to open her eyes, he says.

Stop rushing, be careful, the mother says. And he agrees, although he forgives her this, and everything his daughter does. He watches her pouring orange juice from a big bottle, spilling some, his wife calling out, Stop it, leave it for me. He notices all the cards still on the bookcase in front of his *Purgatorio*. He wishes she'd put them away, but that's her choice. He says to his wife, What's for tea? She says, Olivia, put your uniform out, I gotta wash it before I leave for work. And then she starts chopping carrots, and he asks why the big meal if she's rushed, and tired, but she won't reply.

He goes into the lounge room and sits with his daughter. Settles into the old seat that's his seat, still there, with the big dent his arse makes. She's watching television, and he says, What about homework?

In a minute.

Always in a minute. That's all you ever say.

He watches his daughter. The way she might or might not be a centimetre taller than when he took her to school this morning, her jaw a bit sharper, her eyes keener, her attitude … different. So neat, this little package of person. Not that he can take much credit. What for? Having sex? Reacting with surprise to the announcement? Going to the pre-natal classes? Being there, as this thing, and the other thing (upstairs) came out?

These are repeats, he says to his daughter, but by now she's colouring in an old book. She ignores him. Like he's the Invisible Man, losing his importance, his relevance, his efficacy (a word they used at work a lot). Invisible. Unemployment has that effect upon you. Whereas once you got up early, rushed for the bus, and came home after the fleshy parts of the day had been eaten away, now you were always around and, inevitably, unshaved, dressed in old clothes, and people (even your family) looked at you like you were a leftover screw from some flat-pack that worked just as well without you.

You were sent to do useful things, like pick the kids up from school, shopping (although you always bought the wrong size, or flavour), but that wasn't the same as putting on a tie, which ended in money appearing in your bank account. No matter what you did now, no one gave you money. And although you tried to change this (on a daily basis), nothing improved. No matter how many jobs you applied for (two or three a day), the odd, occasional interview (which always ended with, Yes, we're speaking to a few more people tomorrow), no matter what, you always ended up back in your seat at three pm watching *The Chase* (UK) and *The Chase* (Australia) or some show that required you to pick a box or a number to make your fortune. Then tea, more telly, bed again. Although you'd spent the afternoon lying there. Thinking about how you might stand, clean the bathroom, prune something, paint something. Although you never did. Just studied the dust on the fan, the small crack in the ceiling that you never had or would get around to filling. Eventually arriving at the end of the day, and bed proper, and sleep, where no one could get to you.

He says to his daughter, Homework, perhaps?

Did it all in class.

She always says this, but he's inclined to believe her. It isn't such a great school. The teachers are dim, lazy, always on strike. This is what he's told his wife: We should move her.

Where?

St Brigid's.

Six grand a year?

You can't fuck around with education.

Where? Where do we get that money?

And what she means, with you sitting around watching telly all day.

He's held her accountable to this. He's said, Cos I'm too fucking lazy?

Don't be so precious. I just meant, where do we get all the extra money?

But he's seen it in her face. The way she talks loudly, and only answers certain questions (that suit her).

We've got enough money for school fees. And anyway, they say if you can't afford it, they can arrange remissions.

Well, give them a ring.

As he waits for more, as she just chops carrots.

All of which makes him feel bad. Really bad. Bad husband, bad father. He just kept sending letters, but most employers didn't reply. Didn't acknowledge his application, efforts, attempts to be upbeat and positive (despite feeling the opposite) at interviews. No email, even, telling him he was unsuccessful. How hard was that? A group email, Dear Mr or Mrs whoever, while we appreciate the time you've taken to prepare your application … No, not even that. Like people were footpaths you could squat over and shit upon.

Sitting, listening, he feels this regret. That his daughter deserves more. Although maybe it's him, because when he does raise the topic, and says something like, It's a bit crap, with a house-dad, she just says, So what, plenty of kids' dads are home.

Which makes him feel better, for a while. Until he sinks, further and further, into his chair, so it just opens, and he falls into the PVC darkness, with Larry Emdur in his ear offering a second chance. Sometimes, when he's got nothing to do, he gets in the car and drives to the local IGA and goes in and buys coffee, and returns and sits listening to Frank Sinatra and watching people coming and going. He does this for an hour or more, wearing sunglasses, wiping the tears that come and go without invitation, as he solidifies, and finds he lacks the will to sit up, reach out and switch on the radio, or start the car. Like these things are too much of a commitment, and anyway, how does adjusting your mirror change your situation? The way he gasps for air, and tries to talk himself out of it.

Returning to the kitchen, he says, Need a hand?

His wife says, Fuck, I forgot the mince.

I can get it.

But she just calls, I'll be back in a minute, I forgot something.

Into her car, and he sits beside her and says, What time do you start work?

Although he knows. Ten-fifteen. Then home at six am, school lunches, uniforms, the whole lot, before she crawls into bed at nine and sleeps until the afternoon pick-up. Which is why he feels useful getting the kids when he can. It saves her. And she's trying so hard, struggling, against everything.

As they drive he watches the way she fights the wheel, toots road-hogs, swears, and he says, Calm down, there's no rush.

People are so fucking rude.

You don't want an accident.

Fuck off! Giving some bloke the finger.

He feels bad that she's become this person. Angry, always moving, cursing, like she's at war with the world. Her alone. Although it isn't like that. They're a team. They always have been, since they kissed, and fucked behind the Year Three classroom at Magill Primary when they were only seventeen or eighteen years old. That's how it was back then. When they were just kids themselves and had no worries and she fell asleep as he read her his favourite HG Wells, and they ate nothing but Tim Tams and drank nothing but Coke.

He wants to reach out and hold her arm, and tell her to calm down, but can't, and it's his fault she's so angry. So he says, Why don't you call in sick, although she never does. Because what if she lost her job, and there was no income? Then they'd be fucked. They had enough savings for a few months, maybe they could limit their repayments, but if she had as much trouble getting a job as him (she was a nurse, and there was a surplus) then what about the kids, the holidays, everything?

They go into the IGA and he follows her along the aisles. He loves supermarkets. Like the whole world is here, waiting to be eaten. The cleaning aisle, which always makes him think of home, childhood, exploring shops with his mum. Not so long ago (he is only forty-two). The plastic six-shooters, and the rings of gunpowder. And carrot cake, although they never have it, because he's the only one who likes it.

They return home and she starts cooking the mince for the shepherd's pie. He's never liked this meal, but it's good for the kids, she says. Even Tom will eat it.

Tom. Right. Up the stairs, and the door's ajar. He goes in, sits beside his thirteen-year-old son and says, Homework?

Done.

Tom is drawing. He loves sitting at the window, watching people walk past, drawing caricatures. Like Michael Wright, who's lived in the same house for fifty years but never fixed a globe, mowed the lawn (which has become a pasture), shaved. So that now he is Catweasel, coming out at dusk to buy groceries. Tom sometimes passes him and says hello and Michael greets him with a soft, formal tone, like he's seen and knows everything.

Tom draws Michael with his flowing beard, his Hawaiian shirt open to the tummy (showing his hardened old nipples), his fat legs, footy shorts and sandals. A sort of Latter-Day Jesus in the suburbs, with his house full of books (Tom has seen inside) and the single light that glows throughout the night (as Tom sits watching).

He watches his son's hand moving across the paper. Making small marks, cross-hatching, careful eyes and exaggerated ears. Shading, pushing harder, breaking a lead and sharpening his pencil. He sees how his son's arm is long, without features: no hair, or veins, or scratches. Like he's bought it from an arm shop. He feels proud that his son is perfect in so many ways. His little ball-and-joint shoulders, long neck, smallish nose and brown eyes. Which pleases him. That this boy exists, and always will, for as long as he's around. But also, worried to the point of sickness, as he watches Tom force the tip of the pencil into the fleshy bit between his thumb and fingers, then pick up the razor from the sharpener and start testing it along the length of an artery. Again and again, harder and harder, until there's the beginning of a cut.

Perhaps to distract him he says, Can I help you with anything?

It's done, Dad, scribbling out the drawing, tearing it from the pad and throwing it across the room.

Because he can be moody, too. Maybe this is his fault? Where else could this surliness have come from? Being a teacher, he's always been calm, considered, level-headed.

Anything, I can get it up to an A?

No, Tom says.

And independent. Even when help is offered. Which is a pity, because he knows he can help his son do well at school, as long as he's willing to accept help.

English teacher. It had gone like this: he'd had a good job in a Catholic school in a crap, outer northern suburb, but this one year (2007) they'd given him all of the bad classes. And bad out there was bad: no one worked, handed up assessments, listened to him. One day he'd lost it and held some sixteen-year-old crim against a wall and threatened him, and then the mother was on the phone, and he was in the office explaining himself, and he quit. Like that, without really thinking about it, and his wife had given him the lecture (about their two-year-old son, Tom, and how would they pay the bills, and why don't you ring and get your job back). And ever since then he'd been on short contracts (no one at his old school wanted to risk playing around with the truth) and relief teaching, and unemployment. So that now he was in his forties, and unemployed, and had been for some time, and how did you explain that to prospective employers? When schools were taking on hard-working kids in their twenties who cost a lot less and did a lot more and didn't lose their cool. Now he was an old iPhone. There were too many newer, better ones. Which left him with *The Chase*, and the feeling that he was in some museum of teachers that no one wanted to visit.

Tom lay on his bed.

You tired?

I couldn't sleep … my tooth.

Did you tell Mum?

She said she's booked me into the dentist.

He goes downstairs, past his wife, throwing pots and pans around the kitchen, and into the garden. It isn't in good nick. Weeds, which he used to keep sprayed, the monstera double its normal size, the roses all black-spotted, yellow-leaved. He sits in the old chair he picked off someone's hard waste, reclines in the sun and listens to the shed door banging. He can smell the wisteria (which has overgrown the tool shed). He's never felt the need to keep it under control. It just gives; grows in bad soil; fills the night with the same smell he remembers from aisle eight: Washing Powder.

Again, for the hundredth, thousandth time, he tries to think of where he fits into all of this. He can't see it. He can keep a nice garden, but no one ever comes outside. He can edit an essay or story (and indeed, can write short stories, two published in *Southerly* when he was in his early thirties). He can father, and encourage, and inspire. He can do lots of things. Lots.

Later, he smells the tea and goes inside. His son and daughter and wife are sitting around the table. He sits in his spot and surveys the meal she's made not so much through love, but obligation. Tom says, Sean's dad reckons he can take us skiing again next Saturday.

He sees how happy his son looks – to be going up the river with his mate, his dad (with whom Tom's started bonding), and skiing – something he's never got around to doing. Sean's dad is tall, slaps his kids on the back, calls them shithead and fanny, and they love it. Tom's responding. Just the thought of this bloke fills him with terror. Filling the void of the invisible man. His temperament, his frustrations and pre-occupations, not to mention the money he'd need to buy a boat. Still, once he'd said to Tom, Bet you love the water, and Tom had sensed his (his dad's) regret, and said, Na, it's better when we look at old books.

No?

Yeah.

Perhaps he should have been another sort of man? One who drove a big ute and laid pipes or bricks and made a real go of it, and started his own company and employed dozens of men and made millions, and bought shacks and motor boats and took his kids to Florida.

Tom asks, Can I go?

They'll be getting sick of you, his mother says, and he says, Let him go, because if he can't supply these things, why should the boy go without? As he watches Tom's grin, and smile, when she agrees. He thinks it's funny how there's nothing he can do now to be a better father. Or his daughter, under the sheets, asking this boy, this Todd, to meet her after school at the Plaza. He's seen them, and followed them. Knows what she's capable of, at twelve. Eating away at him, cos he never thought it would end this way.

He always meant to take them fishing, but never got around to it. Standing all day on a jetty waiting for bream to swallow a lure, and the fight, and it'd just get away. Another regret. As he chooses not to eat the pie.

His daughter tells his wife that she's allowed to apply for an exchange visit to Germany, and she has a good chance because she's top of the class, and it will be next year, during the school holidays, and can she go? His wife says, We'll see, but he says, Of course you can, there's plenty of money now.

But he doesn't feel good. He feels he's made every possible mistake, one after another, right up until now. Like he's spent his life flipping a coin and calling heads and only getting tails. But maybe that's the same for everyone? Watching his wife, slowly eating the meal, staring at the wall, he understands. She only ever told him it'd work out. Maybe, he thinks, it reaches a point where you can't stay afloat, or see anyone coming for you, and give in, relax, and wait. The blue of the sky, the cumulus you've lost, the birds, even, circling.

He stands and approaches the bookcase.

In Sympathy.

He studies the photograph. He doesn't look a day over thirty.

As the shed door keeps banging in the breeze.

A perfect day for bream

African Night Crawlers are different to European Night Crawlers, see. They can tolerate extreme conditions, breed ... overnight, you should see, double in size. So if you thread them onto the hook, like so, see ... fish'll go for the wrigglers, make sure they're still wriggling, but you want to know, don't you? It was the same woman, and if I hadn't have acted it could've ended terribly, he wasn't much of a man, a person ... like this, see, they don't have nerves, it doesn't affect them ... It started on a Tuesday. Me and this new junior constable, detective, were sent to this woman's house, horrible, horrid, her lying in a pool of blood and the kiddy, a girl, six or seven, but you couldn't tell because ... well that's the sort of man he was ... like this, I line them up, cast off, within a few minutes, bream, especially, you following, son? What did you say your name was ... Ah, yes, the story, they said it was starting early but you don't pay attention to that, I was, I am perfectly fine ... So the crime scene people take their photographs and gather their evidence, not that it mattered, because I knew, I knew it was the boyfriend, we'd dealt with him before, nasty, vicious man, he'd ... Anyway, the bodies are taken away, there are autopsies, reports, and we start looking for this man, this Roberts, is that the one you've come to ask about? Of course it is ... like this, and it's a perfect day for bream, perfect, would you like to come with me? We can, can't we, if that bitch on the front desk says ... can you do something to help get me out of here, son? Talk to someone? A doctor? They're determined to keep me locked away so I won't embarrass them, cos both you and I know what really happened, don't we? Cos of course, you want to know, they have a million eyes, maybe a thousand, a hundred, do you know, do you know, son ... fair question, what happened next ... Maybe a month passed, and I was down at Thurgoona getting meat, a good butcher there, and I see this woman who was meant to be murdered, but she wasn't, she wasn't murdered by him, and her daughter, the same girl I'd apparently seen on the floor, and they're waiting for a coupla schnitties, and of course I'm shocked, but then I start thinking how, how did this happen ... there's a code on that door, son, and if you could find out ... right? We could go, you and me, down to West Beach, pop a few lines in the water, eh, the crawlers, anything you want, whiting, bream, garfish ... righto, I understand, but the thing is, I didn't overact, I didn't say anything at the time, I wasn't sure what was going on, who was kidding whom, why, was someone trying to protect them for some reason, but it was them, son, the worms, they keep struggling for days and days, so there's no rush, if you could get us a pair of rods we could head out to Semaphore, but shh, don't tell the old bitch we're going, son, and you're a copper, too, you can get the code, can't you? Either way, as I say, I say, I say, old chap, I did my due diligence, looked them up, saw the pictures and my god they coulda been fabrications, couldn't they, I made a few phone calls but everyone said, no, no, what are you talking about, Sid, no one knew, see, everyone pleaded ignorance, so I knew something was up ... shh, come closer, I'll tell you, someone had been playing around with the paperwork ... but I wasn't about to be put off, so you know what I did? I started parking outside their house, watching this woman and this girl come and go, and the partner, a very violent, very dangerous man, son … and I kept an eye on them for months, after work I did a few hours here, there, on the weekends, I was told, they're dead! They weren't dead. I intended finding out, I *intend* to find out, son, I followed her, to protect her and the girl, see, to the shops, I waited outside the girl's school, and all the time, trying to work out … Until, that day … look, son, I think I've run out of worms … can you get me more? The boyfriend, followed her down the road, Bellamy Road, was it, is it, Bellamy, perhaps, and he caught up with her, he was on the footpath, she was … and the girl … early, they said, I'm only fifty-seven, son … and they argued, and he took her around the throat and he was throttling the life out of her, son, I had to act, I had to, so I started the car and built up speed and he saw me too late and stepped back but I took the bastard out … I saved her son, I saved her! And the little girl. And when I pulled up this woman was shouting that I'd killed her husband, and she was punching me and I said I saved you, I saved you from him, killing you, missus … sitting under me wheel, his head sorta, open, the girl screaming, her punching me … and someone said call the police and I said I was the police and look she's safe now, she won't be harmed from him, after all … will she, son? But I'm outa worms. Can you get me some, son? I remember what they look like. What they feel like. Have I told you about night crawlers? We used to … years ago, me and my boy …

Fulfilment

2013

Alice Ratcliffe had a simple job. She loaded packages full of clothes, books, games, discs (and a million other things) into a big cage. When this was full she pushed it up a small ramp onto a landing at the Fulfilment by Amazon (FBA) centre in Moorebank. She applied the brake and ticked a box labelled DELIVERED on a sheet hanging from the cage. All the time, the centre's piped music (an easy-listening rotation with an emphasis on light classics), a spray unit on the wall giving twice-hourly puffs of spruce forest, and cameras following her every move. She waited until a man named Roger (who called her *darlin'*) backed his truck up to the loading bay, got out, pinched her on the bottom and said, 'Should we get going?'

Sometimes, Alice imagined Roger was talking about other things. *Get going?* In the back of his truck. She imagined what this would be like. She'd never known. She guessed, at 62, she never would. But she lived in hope. Once, Roger said to her, 'So, are you married?'

'No.' Blushing.

'Nice girl like you … live alone?' Grinning.

'I live with me brother, Ned, at our house.'

'You live with your brother?'

'Dad's house … see?' She took out an old black and white photo and showed him. It was taken in their backyard, in the late fifties. It showed her father, her, Ned. Roger looked carefully, and said, 'What's that?'

'What?' She checked.

'Someone's been scratched out?' He indicated where – the ghost of a child, or woman, standing beside a monstera. A face, eyes, perhaps, and bits of hands, all that remained from where someone had taken a coin and removed her, or him, or it. 'Who's that?' he asked.

Alice reclaimed the photo, put it in her pocket and said, 'Ned's looking for work.'

'Really?'

'Has been, for a while, a few years.'

'Right ... well, I gotta get this lot delivered.'

This was Alice's life: FULFILMENT. The ramp, the bay, the truck, the drivers, the paperwork (three copies in yellow, blue, white), over and over again. No variation. Nothing. Until one day her supervisor, Gary, handed her a letter and said, 'This is from Geoff.'

Geoff. The boss.

Alice wondered whether she'd done something wrong, again. It'd happened a few times. Most recently when she'd left a carbonara in the oven in the staff room and it had caught fire and there was an alarm and the whole place had to be evacuated. She'd been called into the office. Geoff had said, 'Do you know how the fuck much that's just cost us?'

'No.'

'Lots. Fucking lots. Four engines, three hundred staff standing in the car park scratching their fucking arse cos of you, Alice!'

She'd felt like crying. But she didn't. She wouldn't give him the pleasure. She was sent back to work, but this time, taken off the sorting line and put onto the cages (after Geoff had told her how he'd like to shove her in one). He'd said, 'If it wasn't for that fucking mong subsidy.'

Alice read the letter and said to Gary: 'It reckons they don't want me no more.'

Gary shrugged. 'Were you on a wage subsidy?'

'I reckon. Cosa me injury.'

'Did it run out?'

'Me injury?'

'No, your subsidy.'

'It might've.'

Alice wondered how this might affect her house, her disabled brother, Ned (who lived with her). Whether it might mean she couldn't go to the movies on a Thursday night, or buy hot doughnuts (once a week) on her way to work. Lots of things. Things would change, surely. She went to the staff room, opened her locker, got changed, placed her uniform, her keys, her swipe pass, all of it, on a table. She left the fulfilment centre, telling anyone who might be interested she'd just been sacked. No one cared much. When she got home she opened the door, went inside and called, 'Ned? Guess what they did to me today at work?'

He didn't reply. So she went into his room, and stood in the doorway: 'They said that because my subsidy from the brain place's worn out and all, I'm sacked.'

Not a word from Ned. He was even more damaged than her. So she went out to the lounge room, turned on the television and watched ads (she watched them all night sometimes) for the products she used to put into cages at the fulfilment centre. She got so angry she changed the station and called out: 'Hey, Ned, I'm not buying any of their stuff anymore. Even with that staff discount.'

1961

Ted Ratcliffe had been around the track for years. Firstly, as a clocker, taking times at training (at four in the morning), then as a strapper for Chas Morgan (who'd been put away for some arrangement he had with the bookies), then, for a few months, as a jockey, until he got too big and was let go, then as a bookies' runner. Point being, he'd been around the tracks since he was eleven. He'd got to know the horses, the jockeys, the trainers, the importance of track-work and form and weather and condition. Now, at sixty, there wasn't much he didn't know about the nags.

But in a way, although he knew a bit about a lot, he didn't know much about anything. He couldn't *specialise*. And in an era of specialisation he was finding himself surplus to need. They had a special clocker, and they brought trainers in from interstate, and there were fewer bookies, and they were making less money. And on it went. It wasn't like the old days when he was a kid and you'd get twenty thousand men to the races on a Saturday.

So Ted wrote down everything he knew about racing. He wanted the punters to know what he knew, how to 'Beat The Races' (which is what he called his book). He had chapters called 'Playing the Races' and 'Form and Past Performances' and 'Date, Month, Year, Number of Race'. Like this. Twenty-three chapters in total. 'Weight Carried' and 'Mud Marks'. Then when he'd done this (of a night, when Alice and Ned were asleep), he showed it to a journalist friend and said, 'If you edit the bastard, set it, get it printed, you can have thirty per cent of sales.' Negotiations followed and this friend eventually agreed to forty per cent. Ted wasn't happy, but what could you do? He'd sell millions of copies and they'd both be rich. He said to his daughter, Alice: 'Don't worry about new shoes no more. When this thing takes off ...' Handing her the first copy, fresh off the press.

Alice said, 'Is it a nice story?'

'You bet.'

'Does it have unicorns?'

'Sorta. Unicorns with professional handicappers, if you know what I mean.'

So there's Ted, for the next few months, going from bookstore to bookstore. 'Would you like to stock this one, sir? It's gonna be a big seller.'

'No, thanks.'

Repeated across the city. So he wrote to the big companies – Angus and Robertson, Penguin – and asked if they might be interested in helping him (for a cut) distribute his book. But they all said no.

This is how Ted ended up at Cheltenham Races one Saturday afternoon standing upwind from 'Stinky' Flanagan with a box of books calling, '"Beat the Races". All of the secrets in one book!' With Flanagan and some of the other bookies saying, 'Eh, Ted, take your book and piss off will yer?' But he refused to go. 'Colour, sex, age, pedigree. Thirty years' inside knowledge in one book. Two quid a copy. You, sir, buy this book, read it in a night, you'll never lose again.'

This went on for about six Saturdays. By that time, Ted had sold three or four books (of his four hundred). Enough to make a lesser man give up. But Ted wasn't easily put off. 'The jockeys. Who knows the jockeys better than Ted Ratcliffe? Speed ratings. Track variants. You, sir, why are you giving your money away when you could …?'

On a cold Saturday afternoon in July, three men in suits appeared from the betting ring. One of them picked up Ted's box of books, and the other two stood either side of him and escorted him from the course. Rough handling. Books slipping from box to ground (some miserable bastard scooping them up) as Ted shouted and kicked and threatened to get his mates onto them. At one point they dragged him and his polished shoes ground into the asphalt. They told him he wasn't to return, at least with his books. When he asked who'd sent them they said, 'None of your fucking business.'

When they got to the front gate, Ted was thrown out, onto the ground, and his books were chucked after him. The box came open and the books went everywhere and people started trying to take copies. Ted was torn between shouting at these three blokes and stopping people stealing his stuff. Either way, these blokes (who, Ted guessed, had been brought in especially for the job) stood laughing. He said, 'I've got as much right as anyone.'

'Says who?'

'I've been coming here since I got off the boat. Who the hell are you lot?'

But they just turned and walked away.

Ted asked Harry (who'd been selling tickets for fifty-eight years) if he had a box, and he found one and helped Ted pack his books. As they worked, Harry said, 'You've been making lots of enemies with that book of yours.'

'I'm entitled. Free enterprise, isn't it?'

'Just saying.'

Ted walked across Torrens Road, down Burleigh Avenue, into number seventeen. He dumped his books in the sleep-out and called, 'Alice, Ned, where are yers?'

Alice appeared from feeding the chooks – all perky, all chirpy – and said, 'Did you sell many today, Dad?'

'A couple. Where's Ned?'

'Up his tree.'

'Well, go get him. Tell him we better get the tram to town and see if we can flog a few down Rundle Street.'

1909

The MV *Stella Eden* had strayed too far into the Southern Ocean. Two hundred nautical miles, by the first officer's calculations. He told the captain who, busy entertaining guests, said, 'Well, point her the other way!' A few of the guests laughed. Including Adam Ratcliffe and his young wife, Bertha. Neither had packed appropriate clothing, so their neighbour had offered to lend them theirs. So here they were, at eight at night, in a worn-out tuxedo (Adam) and a long, flowing lacey dress (Bertha). Here they were, listening to the captain say, 'It's not unusual that we'd veer, for a while … with such strong winds.'

'How long do you think they'll last?' Adam asked.

The captain shrugged. 'A day or two. Nothing unusual. She's designed for these sorts of conditions, Mister …?'

'Ratcliffe.'

'You said you were headed for?'

'Mount Gambier.'

'Something about a Blue Lake?'

'Apparently. If it all goes wrong I'll have somewhere to drown myself.' And he laughed, but his wife slapped his shoulder and said, 'You shouldn't joke about those sorts of things.'

There was a nice dinner. Mutton, lamb and three types of fish, although Bertha couldn't stand fish. Yorkshire pudding and coffee, brandy with the purser and another hour's conversation about what to expect in Australia. One woman said, 'Flies. All day. As long as you're ready for that.'

Adam Ratcliffe was a practical man. Life, to him, was a tram timetable. If you studied it, arrived early, you got the best seat.

That's how they'd ended up here, on a ship in the Southern Ocean, while all of their friends and workmates were scraping a living from Lancashire soil (or coal, or cotton). Adam had no intention of letting life tell him how it should be lived. Toil. Early mornings and rough arse paper. But mainly, wise decisions. You could toil, all day, he'd tell his son, Ted, to pull an old cow out of mud. And then what? What would she be good for? Or you could buy a machine. A shiny new machine that sewed leather. You could make shoes, dozens of pairs a day. And you could sell them for five, six times what it cost you to make them (such a machine was still in its box in the hold).

Just after eleven Adam and Bertha returned to their cabin. Three-year-old Geraldine was asleep in her bunk, but eight-year-old Ted was awake, rugs gathered up around his body, knees tight under his chin, a pale face, terrified eyes, saying, 'Where have you been?'

'Get to sleep,' Adam said.

Bertha was over to him, pulling back the sheets, holding him, and Adam said, 'Stop fussing over him.'

'He's all cold,' she said, feeling his skin.

'I went looking,' Ted said. 'I walked along the deck but the man said I should go back to my cabin.'

Bertha felt his wet night-dress, got him out of bed and stripped him naked. He stood in the light of three candles, shivering, his ribs showing, his little tucked-in tummy, his chest with its freckle-sized nipples. White flesh, and purple veins; shivering hands and small, bony legs. Bertha wiped him dry and said, 'You might've fallen over the side!'

'He brought me back.'

'Just get him dressed!' Adam said. 'You fuss …'

Yes, she knew, she did fuss, but Ted was weak. He'd always

been weak. Born at twenty-one weeks, sick for months, crackling lungs and wonky eyes. And it had continued, like this. Another reason, Adam had told his wife, Australia would be good for the boy. Sun. Lots of it. Enough to burn him black like the natives. And meat. Buckets and buckets of meat to put muscles on his arms, and rusty blood in his veins.

Ted was re-dressed, put back to bed, and they all turned in for the night. The ship rolled, port to starboard, stern to bow, and a thousand minor variations. Lifting, dropping, as Bertha said, 'I hope the captain can get her back on course.' Silence, for a few minutes. Creaking wood, and something rolling across the floor. Then Ted said, 'I'm hungry.'

'Jesus!' Adam replied (*his* belly full of cod, and sago).

'It was just biscuits,' the boy said.

Bertha got up, found some bread in the store, gave him some, waited while he ate, while Adam cursed him, then returned to bed. And ten minutes later: 'I gotta go toilet.'

'Right!'

Adam pulled on his pants, his shirt, the tuxedo jacket, approached his son, took his hand and dragged him from his bed. The boy was scared. 'Mama!' Adam said, 'Stop it! Enough!' Shouting into his son's face. 'What sort of person are you?'

Ted was terrified. Screaming. Geraldine was awake, watching her father. 'Stop it, Papa!'

Adam wasn't listening. He was determined. He took a chair from under the table, dragged it and his son out onto the deck, as Bertha, in her nightgown, followed. The rain was coming in horizontally. Pushed by a gale. He dragged his screaming son onto the main deck, threw him down and told him to stay put. Then he placed the chair against the main mast, found a length of rope and secured it. All the time, Ted watching, water in his eyes, in his mouth and ears, whispering, 'Papa!' And further back, Bertha imploring her husband to bring the boy back to the cabin.

But no. Adam lifted his son, placed him in the chair and used the last few yards of rope to tie him down. Across his legs, up over his belly, his chest, until he was firmly lashed, unable to move, still crying for his father to release him. But Adam just returned to his wife and said, 'That should take care of it.'

She told him to release the boy. 'You'll kill him,' she said.

Adam wasn't listening. He was watching his son, his head tossing and falling, straightening, thrown to the side. 'Can't you see,' he said to his wife. 'He has to learn …'

'What?'

'Australia's no place for sissies.' Just watching, a half-smile across his face, spitting water from his mouth, as a purser appeared from the deck above and said, 'Who's responsible for that child?' Coming down, unlashing the boy, picking him up and carrying him back to the cabin. He laid Ted in his bed, asked for a towel and started drying him off. Bertha pushed him aside and said, 'I'll do it.' All the time, both of them watching Adam, who just said (quite unapologetically), 'A bit more of that and he might be good for something.'

Geraldine watched her father from her bed. How he sat on the edge of his own bed, how he removed his wet clothes, how he dried his face in his sheets.

The purser helped Bertha lift the boy's rag-doll body, remove his pyjamas, finish drying him. He turned to Adam and said, 'Were you trying to kill the boy?'

'To teach him … what's it any of your business?'

The purser and Bertha didn't worry about re-dressing Ted. They just covered him with warm, dry sheets, and Bertha rubbed his skin and kissed him and whispered to him. The purser moved the few steps to Adam and said, 'This isn't the end of it.'

'Get out!' He stood – revealing a wide, densely-forested chest, two big tits with muzzle-loading nipples – grabbed the purser by the arms, dragged him to the door and threw him out of their cabin. Then he slammed the door and returned to his wife, to his son, and said, '*This* is the reason we have so many problems.'

She just ignored him. 'He's cold.'

And worse. She knew what it meant when his heart slowed. It meant he'd get ill. A flu. Pneumonia. Weeks in bed. And now, his pulse barely offered anything to the world. A slow, dripping resistance to life.

It got worse. Deep in the darkest part of the night, the ship slipping and sliding across the green-felted ocean, thunder directly overhead, lightning coming in the portholes. Bertha screaming, holding her son in her arms, Geraldine and Adam waking, eyes adjusting, seeing the scene in snatches of light. Bertha said to her husband, 'Are you happy now?'

'What?'

She didn't reply. Just rocked her son's lifeless body in her arms, gathered his hair, smelt it, kissed it, all over his face, small hen-pecks of love that finished with her saying, 'Can you hear me? I'm still here.'

'Is he ill?' Adam asked, coming over, taking the boy's hand, feeling for life. 'He just needs some sleep.'

'Cos he's too weak … are you happy now?'

Geraldine said, 'Should I fetch him some milk, Mama?' Standing close to the drama, so that Bertha could hold her close, pull her into the scene.

A few people knocked on the door. Adam opened it, walked

outside into the storm. The small group (including a man named Jones, owner of the wet tuxedo sitting in a pile on the floor) came into 8H. Jones and his wife saw Ted and asked what had happened and Geraldine spoke on behalf of her mother: 'It's my brother, Ted. He's dead, I reckon.'

Jones told her to fetch the ship's doctor. So she went to the door, past more people waiting to see what the noise was about, along the deck, down a level to the dining room, the library, the offices she remembered from earlier. She stopped a sailor and asked if there was a doctor. He said, 'What is it? What's happened?' She told him she thought her brother might've died.

'Of what?'

'Of being out in the wind, in the cold.' They went up to the main deck and she showed him the mast to which her brother had been tied, the chair, smashed to pieces beside it.

'Where's your mother?' the sailor asked.

'Eight H.'

'And your father?'

Geraldine saw him at the front of the ship (what was it called, the stern, the bow, the port, the starboard?), standing at the railing, looking out to sea. She saw him climbing on some sort of step, pausing, then jumping.

'Papa!'

The sailor called, 'Man overboard!' He ran for a buoy, slipped, pulled himself up and repeated the call. Meanwhile, Geraldine rushed to the spot where her father had jumped, looked into the ocean, but saw nothing except a hand, like it might have been waving, before it disappeared in the swell.

Geraldine and the sailor returned to 8H, stood in the doorway, looked past the people who'd gathered around her brother's bunk. She heard her mother say, 'Some sort of warm mush,' and she thought, she knew this was a good sign. Because that's what she gave Ted every time he was sickly. Warm mush. She shot forward, around a nightdress, under legs, appearing beside her brother's bunk and saying to her mother, 'I went to ....'

Ted moved his head a little, saw her and smiled. All she could think to say was, 'But Papa ...' Before reaching out, touching Ted's cold hand, and feeling it close around hers.

1961

Alice knew her father was drunk. Whenever he was drunk he sang (what he called) the old songs. The songs from England, the place from which he and his sister and mother and father (although he hadn't made it to Australia) had come. Songs from Lancashire. One (that she could hear, from his bedroom) went, '"A beggin' I will go, Of all the trades in England, A beggin' is the best ..."'

She ignored this. She knew, as usual, if things were to be fixed – if her and Ned were to eat, if they wanted new clothes, to go to school, to feel safe – she'd have to *make things good*.

She'd set up a few boxes of her father's books out the front of their house. She'd made a sign that said: 'Beat The Races by Edward (Ted) Ratcliffe for sale £1 today'. She'd sat, for the last three hours, on a small chair she'd found in the shed. And every time someone had gone past she'd said, 'This book could make you hundreds of pounds Mrs (whoever) or Mr (someone).' That whoever or someone had then said (something like), 'Nobody's going to buy a book from you down Burleigh Avenue, Alice.'

A woman called Mrs Pence walked past, saw what was happening and returned a few minutes later with chops wrapped in newspaper. 'That'll have to do for tonight. You okay cooking it?'

'I think.'

'Good. I'll drop by something for tomorrow.'

It was early afternoon when a man stopped and asked about the book, and Alice said her father was the 'King of Cheltenham', and it was guaranteed, if he bought this book and read it and made some *prudent* (her father's word) bets then he, this man, would win thousands of pounds. The man said if her father was so clever why did he make his daughter stand out on the street selling his book. Then, from inside, she heard her father say, 'Nerve of the bloody bastard.' She heard him stumbling about, coming out the front door, down the garden path, out the gate, and saying to this man, 'It wasn't me that told her to come out.'

This man said, 'You're a disgrace.'

Ted took a swing at him, but ended up on the ground, and this man laughed and walked off. Then Alice sat beside her father and said, 'He doesn't know what he's talking about.'

Ted said, 'Don't worry, darlin', we can sell plenty next week at Morphetville.'

She didn't believe him. They'd already tried Morphetville, Victoria Park, the shops on Addison Road, plenty of places. No one wanted to buy her father's book. So she said, 'Maybe there are other ways to make money.'

'How?'

'Like … if you took a job somewhere … I mean, if you like.'

She watched his red, angry eyes swelling and knew she'd said the wrong thing. 'You reckon …?' he asked.

'I just thought …'

She watched his jaw tense, the hairs in his nostrils flare. 'Don't you think I'd do whatever it took to provide for my family?'

'Only Ned …'

Then he exploded. He slapped her across the face, and she withdrew, holding her cheek. He said, 'Since your mother left me to do the whole fucking job …'

Terrified, she said, 'I'm sorry.'

He was burning up. A little artery pumping fury across his face. 'It mighta made plenty,' he said, picking up a book and throwing it across the road. 'And it was all gonna be for you and Ned.'

'I know. I'm sorry.' Feeling the sting. She knew she'd done wrong. Once he got started it was difficult, impossible, to stop him. There was no reasoning. There was no explaining. He reached over, gathered the books and threw them in a box. He carried them down the drive, through the orchard, the dead vegetables, to the chook yard – further and further away from the house. She followed him, not too close, pleading, crying, asking him to understand. He dumped the books in the back corner and shouted, 'Get a match.'

She went in, searched for the matches in the kitchen drawer, her hands shaking. Ned appeared in his pyjamas and said, 'Is he off again?'

She told him to go back to his room.

'What'd he do to your face?'

'Nothing.' Trying to hide it, because she knew Ned had inherited their father's short fuse.

'Enough,' Ned said, and went out the back door.

'Ned!' She followed him. He approached their father and said, 'What'd you do to her?'

Ted pushed him away. Ned fell back onto the grass, but came again, and this time Ted grabbed him and threw him six feet across the yard. Alice tried to make it better by offering her father the matches, but he kicked the boy, hard, in the side. Ned deflated, laid there, without moving. Then Ted returned to the books, knelt down and set a match to the lot. It only took a few moments before they were burning, making a cloud of black and grey smoke that drifted across and consumed Ned.

'What'd you do to him?' Alice said, kneeling beside her brother, shaking him for a reply, as her father said, 'Shh, you'll have the neighbours in here.'

She stood, faced him and said, 'I don't care.' Then she returned to her brother, opened his eyes and said, 'You okay?'

The last thing she remembered was darkness. A hit across the back of the head with a lump of wood that left her, for years to come, slow, retarded (according to the kids at school), a mong.

2013

On the day she lost her job at the FBA centre, Alice sat in her favourite cane chair watching television until seven pm, perhaps a little later. When it was dark and getting cold and her favourite shows had finished, she called, 'Ned, you hungry yet?'

He didn't reply.

She summoned enough energy to stand, went into his room and said, 'We've got chops. You okay with chops?'

Standing in the hallway, or the lounge room, the kitchen, the toilet, you wouldn't have heard a reply. Just Alice saying, 'It wasn't fair, was it?'

Then silence.

'I could put gravy on them if you like?'

Nothing but the sound of starlings from the yard.

'Anyway, I can get another job, eh, Ned? Didn't like that place anyway.'

After dinner, after she'd done the dishes, she took the scraps and went outside, through the orchard, the vegetable patch, into the chook yard. She scattered the tea leaves and egg shells and peelings and bits of old chicken the chooks actually ate. 'Here, chookie, chookie.' Stopping, to look at the two mounds, which (thank god) had flattened over the years. Then she heard a voice saying, 'Thought I better return these.'

It was Mrs Gould from next door with a dozen or so egg cartons. And her dog, Jack, nose to the ground, sniffing about for a feed. Mrs Gould said, 'We've got plenty of eggs, for now, but ... Max reckons you wanted some chard?'

'If you've got it?'

'We've got it. Plenty. He planted twice as much as we need.'

Alice turned and saw Jack digging the second mound with his paws. She said, 'Not there, Jack,' and took him by the collar and tried to pull him away. But he returned, and continued, and Mrs Gould said, 'They treating you better at that place?'

'Yes, thanks.' Anxious. The paws. The damp earth. The growing hole.

'They pay well, do they?'

'Fine.' Trying to pull Jack away again. But the dog returned, and dug.

'Fulfilment? What's all that about?'

'Sorry?'

'Is it about people finding ... *fulfilment*?'

'I guess.' The soil collapsing in a hole.

'Like, something they really want. Something they really need?'

Mrs Gould noticed a bit of paper sticking up from the hole Jack was digging. She reached over, pulled it up, wiped it off and read: '"...critics of the track variant point out ..."' She took a moment, looked at the hole, at Alice, and said, 'So that's where you put him?'

And a second voice, approaching from the old, rusted gate: 'Put who?'

Mrs Gould looked at Ned and smiled and said, 'You know exactly who, Edward Ratcliffe!'

Troubridge Shoals

Anne wondered why they'd come, how she'd pay for the fuel and motel, why she was humouring him. She was pissed off about the two hundred kilometre drive from town, the purple roadhouse with its bra-wall, the girl with the upside down 'Kayesher' badge who wiped her nose on her arm as she bagged their chips. She was unsure of herself, her stand on all this Terry stuff, and she was worried about their small aluminium, tin (whatever it was) boat; two crumbling lifejackets packed beside FRESH GENTS; her eight-year-old son, Jack – buck teeth and roman nose – rowing towards Troubridge Island. 'And what if it's not the place?' she asked him.

'It is … was … will be.' Glaring at her, like she'd lost faith. 'I know it for sure.'

'But you've never been there.'

'I've *lived* there.' His eyes pleading, his brow marked with the bare-backed corrugations of the shoal passing a few feet below them – cool water, copper-coloured seaweed (Jack told her they'd used it for stew), rocks, the occasional bit of wreck (sixty-seven of them, between 1856–1909).

'That was the worst night's sleep I've ever had,' she said. 'Jack?'

'What?' Staring out to sea, to the island, sitting low and unremarkable on the western edge of Gulf St Vincent.

'I said that was the worst night's sleep I've ever had. If they're gonna charge that sort of money …'

'It's not like it's the city. It's not Sydney, it's not New

York' – peering into the spring-clear water, ecstatic dances of red, orange, violet above a budget Noumea, their boat lifting and dropping as the current magnified the smallest changes in hydrography. Spinning, like some sort of sideshow, as Anne waited for the vortex, twenty thousand leagues of misfortune that came from believing in Terry.

Jack gazed into the distance and said, 'I think I can remember ...'

'What?'

'My dadda brought me out here.'

'Your dadda ... Bruce?'

'Yes.'

'Brought you out to do what?'

'Maybe we fished.' Glancing up at her. 'Maybe.'

'So you can remember it?'

He didn't reply. Just pointed to the candy-striped lighthouse on the island and said, 'I told you it was like that.'

'What?'

'Red and white, like that. With the big lens on top. Dadda said it was from France.'

'The lighthouse?'

'*The lens.*' Just staring at it.

'Dadda?'

'Yes.'

'Bruce?'

'Yes.'

'What about *your* dad?'

Jack looked at her like she was stupid. 'He's my dad *this* time.'

Not even that. Jack's father had packed his bags and moved out a few weeks after his son's birth. He'd made some attempt. Brought him home, warmed his milk, got up and changed his nappy during the night – but soon after, after the realisation of what it took to be a dadda, he was gone.

'It's a nice spot,' Anne said, but Jack wasn't interested in small talk. He indicated the island again, growing bigger as he rowed, the sheds and lean-to, the lighthouse, a set of rusted steps surgically inserted halfway up its side. 'Dadda reckoned that before we lived here some ship floundered on the shoals …'

'Floundered?' She'd never heard him use this word before.

'Wrecked. But all the people were fine. And the next morning at low tide they got off and walked over to the island, and this lady, the lighthouse keeper's wife, made them breakfast. I can remember that story.' Smiling at her.

She never felt good when it got like this. When he forgot his Adelaide life – Scotch College, Friday night cubs and Saturday morning soccer. She never felt good. Like she'd lost him, again. Like he'd gone mental, become some other boy. Or maybe he hated her so much he was making it all up. At first, she'd tried to ignore it, saying, 'The sort of nonsense you come up with …' But he'd kept saying it: 'Mum, do you reckon we can go back to where I used to live?'

'Jack, stop that rubbish.'

'What?'

'This island … this lighthouse. You used to live in a lighthouse?'

'Yes.'

Then, after several years of it, after realising her son wasn't joking, she took him to a psychologist, and this man presented several theories, finishing with: 'If you're so convinced, Jack, there's only one thing for it, isn't there?' At first, she'd refused to give in to the silliness. But after so many years of living with two sons – Bruce and Molly in their lighthouse, Terry and his god-damned *dadda* catching sea birds in nets – the suggestion didn't seem so stupid.

Jack stopped rowing and said, 'And what happens if it's not the place?'

'Then we'll know,' Anne said.

'What?'

'That there's some other explanation.'

'Like what?'

She took a moment. 'Like Dr Smith said. Maybe when you were little you saw a movie, an article in a newspaper, a story about a boy on an island. And maybe because you wanted to believe this story ...'

'But,' he said, continuing towards the island (a few Pacific gulls coming out to greet them), 'I actually lived there, I did. There.' Pointing.

'But maybe there's another explanation?'

'No!' He got shitty, rowed as hard as he could, glared at her. 'You're always telling me it's not true, but it is. See! That pen, there, where we kept the chickens. If I'd seen it in a movie why would I pretend? I'd have to be wrong in the head, wouldn't I? And I'm not, am I?'

'No.'

'So why do you always say that?'

This seemed to do the job. He settled. He slowed his rowing. 'That tree's where Dadda would string up a sheep, if we had one, and cut him up for us to eat.'

Troubridge Island sat three metres above sea level. It was part of the sea, the sand, the shoals. Just higher. High enough for a lighthouse to warn ships moving between Adelaide and Perth, a to and fro of barley and iron that helped forge a civilisation built upon its own shifting sands. Three acres of nitre- and saltbush, boxthorn (Jack explained) that kept catching and tearing his clothes (Mumma shouting at him, slapping his bath-bare arse). And birds (everywhere, he'd told his mum): cormorants, gulls and terns, hundreds, thousands of penguins that came to breed. Although she'd become suspicious. The way he listed the flora and fauna in alphabetical order. The facts, like some sort of tourist brochure. One day she found Volume 7 of his encyclopaedia, looked up Troubridge Island, the page well-worn, turned back. Although that didn't prove anything, she guessed.

The small boat from Edithburgh Fish-and-Tackle beached itself on Troubridge Island. Jack and Anne got out and dragged it a few feet up to the spinifex. Anne said, 'So this is where you played?'

He studied the expanse of sand, the scattered pockets of marram grass, an old clothes' line. Anne said, 'Is that where your mum hung out the washing?' But he didn't reply. He walked the few metres to the highpoint of the island and said, 'See … there's hardly none of it. Dadda always said they'd make the light automatic, and they did.'

They studied an iron balcony surrounding the lamp.

'We'd sit up there of a night and watch the ships getting closer.'

'You and your dad?'

'I reckon.' And biting his lip. 'You believe me, don't you, Mum?'

'If that's what you reckon.'

Jack ran down to the beach, checked north and south, called to his mother: 'This way I reckon.' Then darted out of view.

Anne's shoes were no good, so she kicked them off, picked them up, and followed him. 'Careful of snakes.'

'They never had snakes,' he called back.

'They might now.'

A high dune, covered in grass, and he said, 'Maybe it was here.' Turning to make some sort of comparison, before she caught up and said, 'What are you trying to find?'

'Where it happened.' He took off again, and she chased him again, past the ruins of a well, a pile of old steel and wood and bricks, and he pointed and said, 'That's where Dadda put the rubbish.'

'Slow down.'

Now, the beach went out further, presented pools for the sun to warm, a few patches of sea grass, like someone had painted it and wanted to make it believable. Jack turned a few circles. 'This is it. Too far from the house ... I was stupid, Mum.' He stood in front of a small dune. 'This is the one.'

'You sure?'

'I had a spade. I dug a cave because I thought if pirates landed I'd need somewhere to hide my treasure. My salvage. My shells. I dug in till it was cold and dark but then it ... I shouted out ... I told you, didn't I, Mum?'

'You did.'

Even now, she wasn't sure if he was making it all up. The psychologist had a name for it. It wasn't uncommon. And it wasn't that the child needed attention – he or she just wanted to be in a different, better world.

'Dadda said I should always play near the house, but this day I went exploring, and they wouldn't have known where I was. So it was my fault, wasn't it, Mum?'

'No, it wasn't your fault.' She held him close and rubbed his arms. 'Anyway, you've seen it now.'

'I can remember Dadda calling, and someone digging.'

She'd found a box of old VHS tapes, movies, and gone through them, fast-forwarded them to see if there were any scenes of remote islands with boys playing in sand dunes. She couldn't find anything. But he could've read it in a book at school, or seen it on television. She wondered whether this psychologist really understood. 'So what happened next?'

'I don't know … I suppose I was dead by then.'

Strange. And stranger still that he didn't see the problem with this logic. Knowing details, sounds and smells, but not what happened next. 'I guess they got me out.'

'And maybe they buried you somewhere?'

She got the feeling he didn't like this. What did it matter? He'd died, they'd got him out, buried him, he'd gone to heaven or perhaps the realm of Angry Ghosts or Animals, and somehow made his way to her womb, to 7A Stuart Road Millswood. 'So if you don't know everything that happened after you died,' she asked, 'how do you know …?'

'What?'

'You were three and a half before all this began, so something must have triggered it, because you never mentioned it before then.'

He shook his head. He wiped his sweaty brow. 'I don't know.'

'I've been trying for a long time, Jack. I thought coming here would help, but now I'm more confused.'

He held her arm. 'I couldn't breathe. I could feel the sand in my throat. I tried coughing but it went all dark and I remember shaking, and I was so scared, Mumma!'

Anne noticed first. A small runabout, with an old motor that kept stopping and starting, the glint of aluminium off to the west. 'Didn't you say the place was deserted?' she asked Jack.

'They haven't had a lighthouse keeper since 1961.'

They stood in the sun, waiting. As the boat came closer, they made out a single figure, old and wrapped up, grey and bearded, some sort of wet weather cap. 'Maybe we shouldn't be here?' Anne said.

The boat glided through the shallows, the old man reached over and switched off the motor, drifted closer to them. He waved. Anne waved back. But Jack seemed concerned, like he couldn't work out how this man fit into the scheme of his life, his adventure, his revelation. 'He's a hundred years old,' he said, and the old man replied, 'Eighty-six.' Before his boat beached too, he stood, stepped ashore. 'Out for the day?'

'Just a bit of a look-see,' Anne said.

The old man came closer, took off his hat, revealed a mop of white hair. 'You oughta have a permit.'

'Really?' Anne asked. She checked with Jack, but he just said, 'You don't need a permit.'

'You do,' the old man said.

'Anyone can come.'

'Not without permission, son. I'm Barry, and …?'

'Anne,' his mother said, and they both waited for Jack, but all he said was, 'I can come here when I like. I used to live here.'

The old man was confused. 'Live here?'

'Yes.'

'No one's lived here for years. Unless you had a permit to camp?'

'I lived here,' Jack said, loud, defiant.

'And how's that?' Barry asked.

'I don't have to tell you.'

Anne soothed the situation by saying, 'We were in Edithburgh, and they mentioned it was a nice spot, but they didn't say anything about a permit, did they, Jack?'

But he was just glaring at the old man.

'So we thought … the birds, especially.'

'It's a good time of year for that,' Barry said, pushing hair back over his head. 'But the thing is, if you had an accident, got lost, lots of things.'

Jack said, 'Who are you, anyway?'

'I'm paid to look after the place, son. Since the National Parks took over.'

'I used to live here.'

'So you said.' He smiled at Anne. She wondered whether to explain, but realised that would take too long, and the story was hardly believable, to someone like Barry, especially. But it didn't matter, because the caretaker said, 'So when did you live here, Jack?'

Jack refused to be drawn.

'Who did you live with?'

'His parents,' Anne dared.

'Ah, your parents. Who were they?'

Jack crossed his arms, sat in the sand, thought about showing the old man his cave, but decided no, why should I, who the hell are you, *Barry?*

'Bruce something, wasn't it, Jack? And Molly?' Anne said.

The caretaker wiped his forehead with a handkerchief and said to Jack, 'Bruce and Molly?'

Jack wouldn't reply.

'The last to leave in 1961, when the place was automated?' Watching the child. Anne, too. Whatever delicate balance had been formed, was lost. 'Which makes you Blake, their son?'

Jack didn't reply. Anne didn't reply.

'Who went to school in Adelaide and studied engineering, I think. Either way, he worked for BP for years, before he went to live in Hong Kong. So you're him? Blake. Must be nearing forty, eh? Looking good for your age.'

Jack watched his mother. The way her eyes narrowed, her face set hard and unwilling to listen anymore.

'He came back for Bruce's funeral … musta been ninety-one, ninety-two, came out here to see the old place. I showed him around.'

'He says he's some kid called Terry,' Anne said.

'*Terry?*'

Jack stood, said, 'You shouldn't go round making up stories, Barry. I was Terry.'

'*Terry?*' Tilting his head to try and remember.

'I was him, I am, I got killed in that dune and you can't say I didn't because that's not fair, it's not right.' He stood, ran back towards the lighthouse, calling, 'You shouldn't talk about what you don't know.'

Anne said to the old man, 'He was reading some stories about the old place and …'

'Mixed up a bit, is he?' But something was still gnawing.

She knew there was no point explaining. She ran after her son. She slipped in soft sand, fell over, got up and said, 'Maybe it'd be best if you didn't mention it Mr …?'

'Carson. I was just gonna say, maybe Bruce and Molly …'

This time she found hard sand, then grass, and ran along a ridge that led back to the lighthouse. When she arrived she pushed the door open and went inside. Dark, except for light through a waxy window. A small kitchen, and a spot for three or four people to eat at a small table. A few inches of bird-shit crackling under her feet. 'Jack?' She pushed the window open, a pane of glass fell out, fell to the rocks and smashed. The same salty breeze, and squares of sun across her hand.

And from higher up: 'He's making it all up.'

'I know.'

'This is where we lived, up here.'

'Careful.'

Like someone, one day, had just decided to leave Troubridge Island. A few utensils in the drawer, three plates and bowls, a pile of dishcloths, ready for use. A magazine, a story about a boy and an accident with a mangle, how he'd lost both legs but kept working with his father the book-mender. A bowl, and inside, half a dozen shells, a piece of powdered cuttlefish with 'Terry' carved into the back. She held it, examined it, thought for a moment, then called up the cast-iron steps, 'What are you doing up there?'

'Where I slept.'

She climbed up, two treads at a time, stopping to look out the misted windows, until she got to a landing, and three beds set out on old boards. Her son was sitting on a mattress on the smallest, and he said, 'This is where I slept.'

'The old man must have been confused.'

'He's a liar. I know better than anything that I was Terry. You gotta believe me, Mum.'

'I do.'

'You don't. You believe him. You think this kid ... it's not true, Mum, I'm *Terry*.'

At which point he started howling, hammering his face with his fists. 'You think I'm crazy. You think I'm mad.'

'No, Jack.'

Far below, she heard Barry coming into the lighthouse and calling, 'I think I mighta worked it out, Anne, was it?'

'Go away!' Jack shouted. He hit his body hard, turned, saw a hole in the floor, and stepped towards it. Round, jagged, big enough for an eight-year-old. He turned to his mother and said,

'You shoulda believed me.' Then he lifted a foot, floated, and fell. Anne reached out, but she was too late. Just the thump of his body on the concrete, and the old man saying, 'Jesus Christ.'

Anne screamed, ran from the small room, down the few steps, three, four, five at a time. Perfectly regulated, like the tide. And when she arrived she saw the old man staring at her son's body, and blood soaking into the bird shit, his face still and perfect and peach-like. She knelt beside him, ran a hand through his hair, said his name, over and over.

Like this, for half an hour, the old man coming in and out, Anne screaming, pleading with him to fix the boy, the body, the missing father and son and spirit floating, as they spoke, up into the ether, making plans for other worlds, other bodies, other lives. Barry trying to explain, 'I remember, missus. Years before I come here. Some kid they'd lost. Maybe ...'

Soon, it was getting cold, and Anne felt sick and just wanted to lie down and curl up and pretend none of this had happened. Barry tried to move her, take her outside, but she wouldn't go. He knew it was no good, her sitting looking at the body, so he slowly, carefully lifted Jack and carried him from the lighthouse. Thirty, a few more yards. Towards a lean-to where Bruce used to sharpen tools, hang out salted meat, work on bits of broken mechanism. He placed Jack's body in soft sand, in long grass, and stood back admiring him.

Not the place, really. Because there were a few mounds where bodies from shipwrecks had been buried over the years. Mostly nameless, one with a granite headstone that read 'Jackson Parson Asleep in the Arms of the Lord.' Two simple sticks, joined together, with the word 'TERRY' burned into them. 1947–1952. But the caretaker didn't see any of this. He just sat beside the boy, staring out to sea, remembering his wife saying something like, 'They never liked to talk about it … especially after the adoption.'

Eventually Anne came out of the lighthouse. She looked up the hill towards Barry, and the small body beside him. Then she noticed a silver gull, flaring across the sky, settling on the rusted handrail, thirty feet above.

The Sooty Copper

Roland hears someone calling, maybe miles away, wing tips breaking the glassy water, a plane flying low. He knows, if you put all of these things together, they'll describe the world. There'll be some picture you can't see, sitting on a high hill, a hundred yards above the Oder. If everyone could be heard, seen, catalogued, if all the animals could be studied, if all of Herr Klein's equations understood, you'd be smart, wise, rising above the shouting and dramas going on as you lay in bed of a night, trying to get to sleep.

But here's a good beginning. Sitting upstream, watching the river that can still, in places, be crossed in summer. High up, so he can see the birds, the small animals, the insects. He's borrowed Herr Klein's insect jar. He's also taken, without his teacher's permission, his field guide to insects. The plan is to replace both early tomorrow morning before Klein arrives. So it isn't stealing as such. More, extended learning, an extra-curricular adventure. Anyway, he's done it plenty of times before. Klein never notices, and if he did, would probably approve. He's a scientist, too. He believes in the scientific method – hypothesise, test, accept or reject.

The breeze strafes the long grass that runs down to the banks to the Oder. Carrying nice smells, warm oats, baked earth, the trunks and leaves of trees, the scents of flowers. Here, the world sits and waits and lets Roland listen, and understand. Now, for instance. He's managed to catch a sooty copper, asleep on a leaf.

He's looked it up, and made sure. Family *Lycaenidae*. Wingspan 28-30 millimetres. Male black-brown above (Klein's told them this is to blend with the wood), white wing margins, and strange, stripy antenna that he strokes, over and over.

This is what Mama doesn't understand. You don't have to practise throwing grenades, or become a strong, smart, proud German boy to have fun. You don't have to sing about banners flying high, or pioneers on hikes, or learn how to shoot a rifle. Far more important to tell a common copper from a Lang's short-tailed blue.

The voice again, a shotgun ringing out, maybe a kilometre away, the sound of someone playing a saxophone, badly, the sort of pleading, the sort of contentment the oak leaves have as they move in the breeze. All of it. Scooped up, placed in your pocket, ready to be examined microscopically.

He hadn't meant to make a morning of butterflies. If he had, he would've brought Klein's net. But there are so many, in the summer sun, it seems a waste to do anything but study Lepidoptera. Here, for instance, the alcon blue, a dozen circles across its wings.

He looks down to the Oder, perhaps ten metres wide, churned-up water in the shallows, or deep and grey, still and plodding. He knows there's a whole afternoon there. The small fish and crustaceans waiting beneath the rocks. He imagines himself, in an hour, pants rolled up, mud between his toes, dipping Klein's jar into the water in search of tadpoles.

'What's that?'

Shit. He looks up, sees Lena (nine years old, tall, smug, the girl who sits at the back of the class), standing with her arms crossed, further up the hill. He slowly lowers the book, and lets the jar drop between his legs. 'Nothing.'

'I can see.'

He waits.

'You got your pants down.'

He stands, to show her, but then thinks why, who's she, little bitch, always on at everyone about everything. So he sits and says, 'I'm waiting for my brother.'

'You are not.' She comes down the hill, stands a few metres away and says, 'Why you just sitting in the grass, out here, by yourself?'

He refuses to answer. She's a horror. She's smart, and plans her little crusades, carried out (mostly) at lunch with the help of her friend, Mila. For example, they told the new boy, Kurt, that Klein wanted him to run to the shops, buy milk, bring it to the next class. So Kurt appears, halfway through Geometry, holding the milk, and Klein says, 'Where have you been?' Followed by the rant, the strap, the laughs (hidden by hands).

'What are they?' she says, pointing to the book, the jar. 'Aren't they Herr Klein's?'

'Maybe.'

'They are. Why have you got them?'

'He lent them to me.'

'He didn't, you took them.'

'Did not.'

'Why else would you be hiding them?'

Roland takes a moment, decides, then says, 'I borrowed them.'

'Stole.' A smile growing across her face.

'He wouldn't mind. He knows I like insects. Do you?'

She laughs. 'Normal people don't like insects.' She starts thrashing the grass to make sure. 'I better tell him.'

'No.' Sitting on his knees.

'I know what you were really doing.'

'Go away.' Sitting again, opening his book.

'Don't worry, I won't tell anyone. Long as you let me look.'

'Go away!'

'Fine.'

She continues down the hill, towards the stream. 'If you take something it's stealing.'

'I asked him.'

'You didn't. You stole before,' she shouts. 'Remember? The microscope slides? And Klein called your parents.'

'I borrowed them.'

'You borrow a lot of things. But you don't give them back.'

'I do.'

Continuing towards the water. 'Your choice.'

'What?' Standing, taking a few steps.

She doesn't respond. So he runs after her and says, 'You just like to make trouble.'

She crosses the stream on a few big rocks. One by one, carefully. 'Anyway, you don't play with the others. You're weird.'

He waits, deciding if he should go after her.

She starts walking along the bank, in the grass, the bare bits where people fish, over dead wood, the remains of some sort of landing. She stops, leans forward and looks in the flowing water. She takes off her shoes, picks up a stick and tries to reach something. Another step, and another, then she falls, tumbles into the Oder, and the current takes her. 'Roland,' she shouts, but the current has her, and she raises a hand, calls his name again.

Roland stands, shocked, wondering what to do. She'll recover, get out, drip dry, and he can laugh at her. But she doesn't. She travels a few metres in the current, and then stops signalling to him, stops thrashing, stops calling. He takes a moment to think.

So many problems washing away. No, he thinks. It's just so strange, so unexpected. Is he, for example, under any obligation to act? He was just sitting on the hill, minding his business.

She's so far away now, and her body is bobbing in the flowing water, up and down, side to side. He runs, over rocks, the pier, through grass, up a high bank, around a tree growing on the edge of the river. He gets level with her, but she's in the middle, and even when he stands up to his ankles in the water, she's too far away.

She continues, he follows. She's not moving. Face down in the water, her dress sticking to her legs, catching air, ballooning, revealing knickers, all white and frilly.

'Lena!'

But nothing. Just the bobbing, the floating.

This continues for another fifty metres. Eventually she tangles in some half-submerged branches and stops. Up the hill, Roland sees a farmer leading cows along a track. He calls to him, but he doesn't hear. He wonders what to do. Go up, explain, get help? Risk her drifting off again?

No. He can get to her. Maybe she's still alive? Maybe he'll pull her up on the bank and she'll recover and thank him. So he takes off his shoes, his socks, his pants, wades into the water. The mud is cold and sticky between his toes, rocks, years of dead vegetation, and something wriggling. But he keeps going, up to his own hips, reaches out, grabs for her, misses her, tries again, gets her. He tightens his grip, manages to pull her free, but she jags, and he struggles with her arm, her weight, the current. Now he's got both hands under her arms, and returns to the bank, dragging her through the mud.

He rolls her over, pats her on the back, hard, harder, and says, 'Cough it up.'

But there's no coughing.

So he puts her back down, studies her pale face, the blue around her eyes and nose and mouth, her bloodshot eyes, and the way her tongue hangs from the corner of her mouth. Then he sits back and thinks. Dead? He shakes her again, calls her name again, checks her pulse, like Mama did when Opa died. Her flesh is chilled, pasty, covered in fine capillaries.

He doesn't feel any pleasure. He doesn't feel any vindication. He does feel happy that Herr Klein won't find about his book. He just sits, his legs cold, his underpants and legs covered in mud. All of this seems strange. From the sooty copper, to a corpse. He wonders how he'll explain it. *I was sitting in the grass, and she was crossing the stream, and fell in …* Strange, perhaps, that he was there, at that time, so close, saw it all, couldn't save her. There'd be plenty of questions, and although he hasn't got any guilt, although he wasn't involved, people will still ask. Where exactly were you standing? How long did it take to get to her? Remind us, what was your relationship? Hadn't you two argued in class, in the yard? And more than this. What about the way her parents (he tried to avoid her grey face) would look at him, and speak to him? What would her sister say, what would she do, the neighbours, relatives, the whole town? A small girl had drowned, and he hadn't saved her.

So he pushes her away, grabs her ankles and drags her towards the water. When she's far enough in, he rolls her a few times, and she plops into the water with a little suck of air, then floats away.

Damn. The bank, with its drag marks, its indentations. So quickly, he tries to rub it all out with his feet, goes into the water, splashes around, rubs again, splashes again, until he's happy it doesn't look like a crime scene. Then he takes his socks and shoes and pants and continues along the bank, following her. Now, he prays she won't get caught again. He asks himself, if she does, whether he'll go in again. All of this going through his head. How to commit the perfect crime he hasn't committed.

Grass. Mud. Tree roots. A ford that, luckily, no one's crossing, that's still deep enough to allow her body to keep drifting. Then, a voice. 'It's a kid.'

He drops to the ground, crawls into the long grass, sees a man and his teenage son come down to the river, stand watching Lena for a moment, before the man takes off his shoes, jumps in and swims towards the body.

The boy just watches. 'Can you get her?'

He can. He gets her foot, her leg, takes her under the arms and starts swimming back.

Right, I'm free, Roland thinks. He crawls through the grass, up the hill, until he's on the other side, then he stands and listens and hears the man (he's good at picking sounds from a distance) say, 'Quick, get Gert, tell her to send help.'

Roland runs, five, ten minutes, at speed, through a copse of trees, along the edges of farmers' fields. When he feels he's gone far enough he climbs the high bank, runs down, swims across the river, drags himself out, and sprints to his starting point.

Eventually he finds his spot, spreads out his pants, his shoes, takes off the rest of his clothes and drapes them across the grass to dry. Like this, for an hour. Soon his body and his thoughts settle. None of this was his making. None of it's his fault. He tells himself this, over and over. Eventually he picks up his field guide, turns to the next page and continues.

The boy in time

Seven months

The voices, distantly, but the boy can't make them out. Papa says, 'Where do they come from?' The boy (who's sitting in his small, hand-made cot) knows he's talking about the black cloud, although it's not a cloud, it's not smoke, it's nothing like this, it's *insects*, so small they look like a cloud, but they're not. They have small bodies, made of even smaller parts, and if he catches them (he often does, sitting here overlooking the ocean) and crushes them they turn red on his fingers. This is what's annoying Papa now, waving his hands instead of laying egg wrack on the slats where it dries before he gathers it and takes it to Mr Scott who gives him money and this money buys bread and mutton and he, they, the whole family eats it. Just Papa saying, 'What's to be done about it?' Mama asking what then, tell me. These are the sounds of his life. Or these: *Atlantic* waves crashing on the beach, on the rocks, near where Papa keeps the boat in which he and Terry go out to fish; his *parents* arguing, sometimes singing, sometimes whispering so he and Terry (he guesses) won't hear; the fire in its place; the mutton birds that land close to the house and pick at what's left on the ground. There are other things, but these are some of the things he sees and smells and hears every day, sitting in his cot on the porch of their small cottage with its smoky fire.

And seeing. He's seen it all! He's seen the whole world in *Barra*. He's seen, he sees, every day, a big, blue sky that stretches from one side of his world to the other; he sees a small, white cloud, and wonders where the others have gone, and later, sees lots and lots of clouds piled black and blue as the bruises on his mother's face; he sees the tree in their yard moving in the wind that comes off the sea his father and brother fish. He sees three sheep in their yard, and Mr and Mrs Scott and the Braithwaite twins coming for cream; he sees Terry's face watching him, talking to him, saying words like *shat yerself* and *pudding-boy* and *hungry, are yer hungry again*? And smell. He smells himself. He smells his shitty arse, and a smell that's everywhere all the time, and guesses this is the smell of the sea and the wrack and the dead fish and boiling mutton and cabbage and his father's hands and his mother's breath and knows all of these smells add up to whatever his world is. And there's Papa now, still waving away the midges, and he thinks how can there be so many of them, and how can they be born and shit themselves and grow up to be Terry then Papa then old Mr Braithwaite who was buried in a hole on the hill as the Allasdale choir sang *My redeemer liveth!* ... then die? How can each of them live this life? They can't. They must live a different life. They must fall out of the tree and fly about and get angry and busy and just fly, fly and then die and fall to the ground and make a mess that Mama has to clean up as Papa says enough of this dung heap of an island! And now the midges are in his mouth and he spits them out, and the singing gets louder, and he can hear *Lord your summons echoes true* ... And Terry's face again, watching him, then Mama, saying, 'The water's ready.'

Terry pulls the boy from his cot, lays him on the table, removes his nappy, his shirt and singlet, all of it – then he's cold, because it's never *not* cold on Barra (he's heard plenty of people say this), and it's never not raining or windy and why the hell do we live here, are we stupid, it's time we looked at moving to Australia, Mother. All of this aside, it's unpleasant lying on the table in the cold, with Terry saying you stink, you little monster, but he doesn't care, he just kicks his legs, he loves kicking his legs, hard, harder, like he's bruising the air and the world around him, though he's not. Terry picks him up and calls him a pudding boy and places him in the bath and the water is too hot, and he starts crying and Mama comes over and tests it and says wait and gets a jug of cold water and adds it then it's better, and he stops crying. Terry picks up the rough, sandy soap that's made from the seaweed they gather from the rocks, and he, Terry, starts rubbing the boy with the soap and it makes bubbles and smells nice and the boy feels clean. Terry holds his fat legs, his *feet*, and cleans between each *toe*, cleans his *belly* and *bottom* and *back* and *neck*, all of these words for each bit of his body. Meanwhile, he's watching Papa lay wrack on the slats, carefully, slowly, like it's something important. He likes wrack. Sitting feeling it, the little eggs, crushing them like he crushes the bugs, and they, too, burst, but instead of leaving red they leave salty water, and he tastes it and spits it out and Mama and Terry see this and laugh and take it off him. But wrack is important. It's everywhere, it's all around them, it's on their hands and in their clothes. Like someone, the God they sing about, has given it to them as a gift. And the voices coming from the sea, from the small boats that come every Sunday for church, sing: '*Will you set the prisoners free …?*'

He's not sure who these prisoners are. He knows Mrs Braithwaite was killed by a man who *became* a prisoner. So maybe this man should be set free? Maybe God can set him free? Either way, this is what they sing as they approach the island. And now, as happens every Sunday, a few people in the cottages along the coast (including Papa, still busy with the wrack), sing back to these people: *'Will you kiss the leper clean?'* And the reply: *'... and do such as this unseen?'* He's not sure what any of this means, but he is sure the people in the boats are singing, and his people are singing back. Like they're saying hello to each other, but that doesn't matter, because now Terry has finished cleaning him and takes him from the bath, lays him on the table, starts dressing him in the outfit he wears to church on Sunday. Lying back, kicking his fresh, clean, warm, fat legs, and Terry holds them and says, 'I can't dress you if you won't sit still.' But he doesn't care, he kicks, and his mama comes out and holds his legs and between them, they dress him. Papa says, 'I won't go if he's there,' and Mama tells him to stop being stupid, but he says, 'It's not me that's stupid.' The boy knows they're talking about Mr McLennan, because they always sound like this when they talk about him. About how, if they had the money Mr McLennan owed them, they'd be fine, they'd be set, and if he doesn't cough up I'll take things into my own hands, Mama telling Papa don't be so ridiculous, Papa saying, 'It's theft, and it's not just me, Agatha.' Her telling him the man needs more time, Papa saying six months is long enough, and he has money, plenty of money, don't believe what he says.

It's a day called September 8. He heard Mama say this morning. He saw her consult her Book of Saints, tell them it's the birth of Mary, a day to think the best of people, to see God in the eyes of strangers (though Papa grumbled). Then she told them about Nazareth and Joachim and Anne, and the boy, sitting listening, wondered how these words came from the book. Like it was magic. Like the insects came from the sky or the trees or the clouds. Who knew? But she seemed to be getting this story, the life of Mary ('the chosen one of Adam's race') from the pages she kept turning, the lines she kept following, and he thought, perhaps, everything in the world is in this book, and maybe the other two books in the bookcase. One is called the Bible. The other has pictures of a place called Australia, and Papa keeps reading it and showing Mama and saying (things like) we can at least enquire. Look, nine at night and they're still on the beach ... a day that's a hundred and twenty in the shade. Bugger this! But she won't bugger it. She loves the rain and wind and daily blessings from the saints and mutton and potatoes, every day, potatoes, and the fish her husband brings home in the boat, all of this. So there are three books. And sometimes he cries for them and Terry gives him *The Land of Golden Plains* and he sees the people in this country (because there are other islands beyond Barra) have not three, not three hundred, not three thousand, but three million sheep (however many that is). Anyway, Mary's birthday is special. More than anyone's. He's never had one. Although he must have been born. He couldn't have fallen from the sky, or a tree, like the midges. Maybe he'll have one soon. With cake and ale, like Papa's birthday.

The boats from the outer islands are in the shallows, and the boys are rowing, and the old people sing: '*Will you go where you don't know ...?*' Mama and Papa sing back: '*... and never be the same.*' He wishes he could sing, but he doesn't know what to sing, or how to learn, like the old people have. Maybe it's all in one of the books about God and saints and *Sydney*. All he knows is that he's ready for St Michael's, and his brother has powdered his bottom, and he sits up and sees the sky is full of clouds, and some of them are dropping water, and the people in the boats come ashore and the singing stops. Papa sees Mr McLennan and says, 'I'm staying home,' and Mama says, 'If it's that much a problem, I'll talk to him.' Papa says what good will that do, and she says well, what would you have me do? That's the end of that. Papa goes inside to put on the suit with the holes in the knees and Mama puts the boy back in his cot and says, 'That man will be the death of me.' He hopes not; he knows he needs his mother, he needs all of the old people who are coming up the beach towards their cottage. But he wonders, if Mama dies, if they'll put her in the book with the saints, because sometimes she says (something like), I'd have to be a saint, or Bless me, or Lord have mercy on me! Then when he learns the words he'll be able to read about his dead mother, although he'd prefer a live one.

The islanders have come up to the house and Mrs Martin is squeezing his cheek and saying another half-pound, I reckon, and he thinks this funny, because how could the midges put on half a pound in two weeks? They'd all be like kangaroos (he's seen them) flying around in the air above the wrack, and they'd fall out of the sky, and can kangaroos fly? Either way, the singing has stopped, the talking, the bath is emptied on the turnips, his father emerges ready for church and says to Mrs Martin, 'Not a word to him,' and she says (looking at Mama), 'He's got the gout today.' Papa smiles and says, 'Can a man die of gout?' Mama slaps his arm and says, 'Enough of that … on Mary's day!' Papa tells her he doesn't care which day he dies. Then they set off up the hill towards St Michael's. Mama carries him. The sky, clearing again, and the birds, and the older boys and Terry chasing each other and slipping in the mud. All of this.

1.

John Drake sets off from the boat with his sons. Terry, three steps ahead, and Samuel in his pram. Not that the boy can't walk, doesn't have strong, pudding-fat legs, can't run, even. But

John's in a rush and doesn't want to waste time dilly-dallying around Castlebay. So they walk up Pier Street, past a grog shop, the food co-operative, an old woman who sits in the sun carving small girls from soap, dressing them in clothes she's sewed, placing them in a window for all to see. John calls to Terry to slow down, and he stops and waits with his hands behind his back. Papa says to the boy in the pram, 'Try pushing yerself up a hill sometime.' The boy doesn't understand. How can he push himself? He can walk, but his father won't let him, so he stares across the bay, the little castle on its island, walls defining what nature failed to make clear. Maybe someone's dead inside? Maybe they're cleaning fish? He doesn't know and doesn't care, but he does like Castlebay, and they come here often enough, and the roads are narrow and muddy, and there are ruts where the carts get caught and someone gets off and curses God for this bog-hole of a town, and if Papa is listening he says you can say that again (or something similar) and the man gets on and whips the horse till it pulls free. The houses and shops defining the street, people gathering and talking, fishermen with big, brown beards and *sou'westers* and leather boots. Castlebay (the only town he's ever been to) seems the biggest place on Barra, in Scotland, in the world perhaps, but he knows it isn't. Now they have another book called *London: City of Empire*, and there's no city (Castlebay doesn't come close) like London. He often sits and reads it, slowly, page by page, thinking one day he'd like to go there.

John stops, lights a cigarette, and calls to Terry, 'If I have to keep asking ...' Terry says what? The boy thinks this seems *rude*. He wouldn't be rude to his papa, but it doesn't bother Terry. And this is why they've come to Castlebay, again. To say sorry to Father Morgan. His papa calls, 'You'll know about it when you get home,' and Terry smiles and says know about what, and Papa draws back on his cigarette and says to him, 'Make sure you don't turn out like him.' Indicating the seven-year-old, running along Pier Street, up the hill, across the road, another cart having to brake to avoid him, and John calling, 'Terry!' But the boy doesn't care. The boy tries to think how this place is like London. The homes on top of each other, people living in little slices of sky, coming downstairs to cook kippers, toast bread and drink tea. There are horses, like the horses that guard the Queen. A stall at the top of the hill (they're approaching) selling flowers and turnips. Just like London. But that's about all. No palaces or statues or soldiers or theatres, none of this. He's been born somewhere his father calls *the arse-end of the earth*. A place to be gotten away from. His father's still planning this. He's started a file, and the first page of the file says 'Melbourne', and he's torn pictures and articles and sent for postcards of Melbourne. As well as this, he's found a map of Melbourne and indicated some of the areas they might live: Hawthorn, Richmond, St Kilda, like their St Kilda, minus the seals and songs and pints of bitter. So it's clear. Melbourne. Now, his father's explained, they just have to find a way to get there. If he works hard, saves, borrows money from young Mr Braithwaite (he knows he'll pay it back), then one day they'll be off, and there won't be any more boggy roads or soggy rugs from where the roof leaks.

They turn off Pier Street. There's not much here, but the boy loves this place. He thinks, although Castlebay and Barra aren't London, London isn't Castlebay or Barra, and who's to say what's best? This place has everything (Mama keeps saying). Fresh fish from the ocean, stew with potatoes and mutton, books, four books now, and a school where the boys run about at lunch (he's seen them) singing, '*Going home to Rosy Malone, she's the girl with the golden eyes ...*' And soap dolls and fishermen standing in front of the pub with their drinks, each poking him and laughing at his fat legs and saying he oughta learn to fish, and how can a man make a living from seaweed? And the gulls swooping low and him reaching out to touch them, but he never can, and now he tries to climb from the pram and says to Papa, 'Walk up the hill,' but he says no, we're in a rush, we need to be back by four, and pushes him back down, but he struggles, he wants to get out and explore the little lanes, run down to the sea and jump across the rocks, splash in the pools like he does at home. Instead, he settles into his pram, because he realises his father's having a *tough time* with Terry, already waiting in front of the Star of the Sea, calling, 'Should I say sorry to him now, Papa?' Papa says wait, wait, (and whispers) you rotten child. The boy hears this and knows his father doesn't hate Terry, or think he's rotten. It's just something he says.

They stand in front of the church, and Papa says to Terry, 'You know what to say.' Terry does. Mama made him practise: 'Dear Father, what I did to the hymnal was unacceptable and I am working to earn money for its repair and I hope you will forgive me and not think bad of me because I didn't stop to think what I was doing and I'm not normally like this and will God see it, will he, will he be angry, can you pray for his forgiveness because Mama has made me pray already, over and over (after she slapped my legs) and now she reckons if I don't do such a thing again then Jesus and every saint in her book might forgive me ... perhaps.' Terry is standing in his Sunday best (though it's Tuesday). With his hands behind his back, his head looking down at the cobblestones in front of the church, no smile, nothing, and he moves dirt with his good shoes and Papa says stop it, just have a bit of respect, got it? So they go inside, and the church is candle-lit and smoky and there are books, hymnals, plenty of the them, and he wonders whether he can have one to practise his reading, but considering what's happened with Terry, probably not. There's a big Jesus up on his cross, he's heard this story over and over, about how the Romans nailed him up because they didn't believe in love and God and goodness. An altar, but the silverware is missing. Maybe Terry took that, too? Maybe that's also why they're here? Either way, his papa calls, 'Father?' The words spread out, fade in the banners of Peter and Paul, and it's like all of these men, these twelve men, are the fishermen who stand in front of the pub drinking bitter. But they're different people. The Jesus people were years ago, and some of them fished, but most of them followed Jesus and wrote down what he said so there could be a Bible and book of saints. That's how it worked, how this place works, with its candles on the walls leaving soot on the stones that hold up the big roof with the tower and bells and arrow saying where's south, where's London, where's Melbourne? His father repeats: 'Father?' Then he takes the hymnal out from under the pram, hands it to Terry, and Terry opens it to the page where he drew pictures he oughtn've drawn (Jesus with no clothes, and a thing sticking out), and Papa says, 'How are you going to feel, explaining?' Terry shrugs. He says he was bored, but Papa says we all get bored, you have to learn to – But it doesn't matter, because Father Morgan (dressed in a suit, nothing like on Sunday) walks towards them, extends his hand, thanks John for coming, admires the boy and says he's putting on weight, but look, that cowlick will follow you through life (as he tries to flatten it), then turns to Terry and says, 'So what do I owe the honour, Master Drake?'

The boy likes Father Morgan. He's like the fishermen who say the words Mama's banned Papa and Terry from saying. The priest takes the hymnal from Terry and says, 'I was wondering where that had got to.' He looks at the drawing, and the boy can't be sure, but he thinks he smiles, then he looks at Terry and says, 'You've got quite a talent.' Terry shrugs again, Papa pokes him again, and Terry starts reciting the words Mama has taught him, but Father Morgan stops him and says, 'What is it you've drawn on him, Terry?' Terry looks, to be sure, but dares not say. Father Morgan says, 'I'm sure he had one … we're all born with one, aren't we, Terry?' Who shrugs. 'Which means that Jesus, according to your picture, was a man like any man, except …?' He waits for Terry, then says, 'He might be anyone you passed on the way here? Mrs Michaels, McAllen, was she out?' Papa tells him yes, she was carving her dolls, and Father Morgan says, 'That's easy,' tears the page from the hymnal, says, 'I'll keep it to remind you, one day, when you're your father's age.' Papa pokes him again and he continues his apology: 'Mama says she'll buy you a new one and she slapped my legs and there was a big, black bruise and she said that'll teach you ...' But Father Morgan just turns to Papa and says, 'You still planning on leaving, John?' He says yes, Melbourne or Sydney or Adelaide, when he can get the money, and the priest says, 'It won't be a patch on Barra.'

Walking back to the pier, with some sense of relief, Papa allows them to run across the grass, stop and take off their shoes and socks, go into the water up to their knees. Now that Papa can't hear, Terry says, 'There isn't any god, and that's what they're worried about.' The boy disagrees. There must be a god. Why else would so many people have written books and built churches and taught children, millions of them, if it wasn't true? Terry says, 'So they can keep you living in places like this and doing what they say, and making you pay, every Sunday.' Then leaning forward to him (as Papa calls come on, let's have yers!), he says, 'And them Jews chopped off their kids' willies.' The boy doesn't get it. He says, 'All of it?' Terry says yes, well, most of it, they chop them off, so who wants to believe in a Jesus with half a willy? The boy thinks about this. Their Mama, Father Morgan, none of them have mentioned willies. He says why, but Terry shrugs. 'If anyone got close to mine I'd punch him.' The boy agrees, he would, too, and Papa calls, 'Quick, we'll miss the ferry.'

2.

The boy lies in the machair surveying the sky, and says, 'Mama is called *Ag-a-tha*.' The older boy, the boy with red hair and dots on his face, says, 'Mine is called Morag.' The boy decides he doesn't like this name. *Morag*. Like some sort of disease, or monster, or the thing that killed Edward Big Boy. He says, 'Papa is called John.' This time the other boy doesn't reply. So the boy (pointing at the clouds) says that one is an elephant. The other boy doesn't care about clouds. He picks the heads off orchids in the shoulder-high grass, throws them at the boy and says, 'You talk funny.' The boy says he does not, and what does he (he's called Thomas) mean by that, and Thomas makes a strange lispy sound and says, *'My name is Sam, and my papa is John, and my mama is Ag-a-tha.'* Then he laughs and throws more flowers and the boy says what's in Canada? Thomas says plenty of things. Spruce forests and mooses and cities with big schools and lots of things, not like this shithole, imagine having to stay here all your life. The boy says we're not, we're going to Australia, and Thomas says Canada is better than Australia, and the boy says why, why would you say that, and Thomas says Australia is too far and you can't come back. The boy says that's not right, you can, then he points to the elephant that's now a bear and says,

'My brother is Terry.' Thomas says he knows Terry, he's in his class, so why would the boy tell him, unless he were simple, are you simple, Samuel? Repeating, '*Simple Sam, Simple Sam, here I am with Simple Sam.*'

Papa has sent them out to play while he and Thomas's father, David, have a farewell drink. He's explained it like this: when a man goes to Canada he's unlikely to return, and if that's the case, it's like he's died. At which point the boy said, 'But they might come back and see us,' and Papa said, 'That never happens, does it?' The boy thinks this is true. Other people have left for Canada and South Africa and none of them have returned. At this point, Thomas and David were at the door, and the boy thought it funny that David's daughter and wife weren't with them, because they'd all go to Canada and they'd never see them again and wouldn't that be strange? People who live and die and we never see them again, almost like they've never existed. He thinks of another thing Papa said, this time when Mrs Danvers died: 'So now she disappears from history.' This idea stayed with him for days. So after Mama, Papa, Terry, Thomas, David, Father Morgan are gone, it'll be like they were never there, and maybe their kids will remember them, and maybe their grandkids, but that's it. For the hundreds, thousands, millions of years the earth has and will be here (according to Papa's book). Gone. Like the clouds breaking up and making new pictures.

He takes a photo out of his pocket, flattens it on the machair, says to Thomas, 'This is my grandpapa.' Thomas lies down, says it's warm in Canada, you can cook eggs on the sidewalk, but the boy doesn't care about this, and says, 'He was called Karl.' He's angry that Thomas won't look at Karl, so he holds up the picture and says, 'He looks like me.' Thomas shrugs, bites a stem of grass, says a bit, I guess, and the boy says no, a lot, can't you see, and holds it up again, but Thomas says so what if he looks like you? The boy thinks damn it, I'll never see Thomas again, he'll be in Canada, so he can't laugh at me or not believe what I'm about to tell him. 'This is a picture of me. See, me, look' – pointing out the same mouth, the same hair – 'and it was me that was him, and I was living on Barra a long time before I was born.' Thomas sits up and says, 'You think you were your grandpa?' The boy says he knows he was. Thomas asks how he knows but the boy can't tell him, so he says, 'It's obvious.' Thomas asks how, how's it obvious, and if it were, couldn't he explain, but the boy says he can't explain, he was Karl, his papa's papa, which means he, his papa's son was his papa's father, and that might sound strange, but it's true.

Further up the hill, Terry emerges from the cottage, calls, 'Sam, Thomas, come in now,' and goes inside. Thomas stands and says, 'But someone must have told you. Do you think it was Jesus?' The boy says no, it didn't happen like that, and wishes he hadn't told him. The tall, red-headed boy runs through the grass, up to the cottage, goes inside, and the boy is left alone with the photograph he stole from Papa's drawer. By now, he guesses, Thomas is telling them what he's just told him, and Papa is saying, Don't worry about him, he's simple, and his mother's defending him, saying he's not simple, he's just prone to *flights of fancy*. So the boy doesn't want to go in, but again, his brother is standing at the door calling him, so he drops his head low, lower, so he can't be seen and runs his hand through the sand and broken shell in the machair and thinks all of this took millions of years to make and in the meantime who was living here, who was feeding the sheep, who was cutting the wood for the fire, who, who?

Terry again, so he stands, walks up to the house, goes into

the smoky darkness that always has and will be, the candles making soot that sticks to the walls that have and always will be, the fish waiting to be cleaned. Mama sits beside Papa. He can smell their whisky. Terry, at the table, doing sums. David and Thomas watching him, still, and he wonders what he's said about him and Karl, and Papa says, 'How would you like to be going to Canada, Sam?' The boy says that might be alright, but where, Winnipeg, Ontario, Toronto, and David says that's impressive, and the boy says it's all in this book, and reaches over and pulls their seventh book from the shelf and shows them *A World Atlas for Children*. He opens to a map of Canada, and David says, here – pointing – the Yukon. As the boy sits in his small, wicker chair, his papa says to David, 'That's the bit I don't get. It's just as god-forsaken as this place,' but David tells him it's different, because they won't have to burn dung or marry their cousin and have one-eyed children. They will be in the world. They will be in time. They will be involved. The boy thinks this strange. In what way are they, the Drakes, living here on Barra, *not* involved with the world? But this is too big a thought, and he abandons it and says to Thomas (perhaps as a way of making sure he doesn't mention Karl), 'Mr Seabiscuit' (Smith, but they call him Seabiscuit behind his back) 'won't have no one to teach who's eight.' Thomas says, Well, this way he can spend more time with Karl, can't he? The boy thinks shut up, it's not yours to tell about, I shouldn't have trusted you, and his mother says, 'You haven't been going on about that again, have you, Sam?'

Agatha and John are worried about their youngest son. Worried that he'd think this, say it, believe it. Again, they've asked him where he gets such an idea and he hasn't been able to explain (he's not sure himself), so they've said such a thing can't happen, why do you think this, Samuel? Him shrugging. Perhaps, they've worried, it's like the French girl who saw Mary, who thought she *was* Mary, or worse, maybe their son has something wrong in his head, maybe he's slow (but he's not, he's smart!), maybe he's like the man who was also called Karl who lived somewhere in the isles a hundred years before, maybe longer, and who was smart but incredibly stupid, and stole a boat and sailed across the sea and washed up on a beach and the people who found him thought him a merman. Or maybe he's playing a joke? It's too much for them to understand, but they've said to him, stop being stupid, how could such a thing happen, that's storytelling, and you, my boy, have work to do! But it persists, and keeps happening, embarrassing them in front of David and Thomas who'll go to Canada and tell everyone about the strange little family from Barra whose son thinks he's his grandpa.

The boy knows he's Karl. He knows everything about Karl, how he loves Amanda, and his boys John and Robert (who died at seven, and he can tell them everything about the day Robert fell overboard and he went in for him but got to him too late and pulled him out and he was as blue as the sky's blue and he wouldn't breathe and he shouted and screamed and cried). He can recall being a boy himself in the same school with a different teacher and it's many years ago and he's made to go outside and scrape mud from everyone's boots, and he has to do this in the wind and rain and wonders why me, why do I have to do this, what did I do wrong, and he remembers the day they found Harris's son hanging in the pub and they had to cut him down and he sat there and watched and couldn't believe how or why he'd done this because he was brilliant and funny, but dead, and gone from history. Anyway, there are hundreds of things like this he remembers. Some in this hut, some in Castlebay, some at school, but all of them real, and he's told Mama and

Papa but they've said how could you know, you're making it all up. Sometimes he wonders whether he has overheard these stories, and somehow they've stuck in his brain … but when did that happen? From whom did he hear the stories? From ghosts? What ghosts, when, where, how, while he was watching the clouds change, while he was sleeping, he doesn't know and he wants to understand but he can't and when they tell him he's not right in the head it makes him sad and angry at the same time.

So now he apologises to David, says he made it all up for his book, and David says what are you going to do when you grow up, and he says he's not sure yet, maybe collect wrack like Papa does. David says to John, 'Get yerself to Australia. You don't want these two doing what you do.' Papa says it's honest work, but you're right, another year, and David says you said that a year ago, and before that, and you've just gotta go, John, there's no good time … The boy doesn't understand. There's nothing wrong with Barra. It's a nice place. A place he feels like he's been in forever. He can't imagine living in Melbourne. Who would he be then?

3.

The boy lies on his back. On the sand. On a cold, windy morning. He sees gulls and pretends he doesn't know they're gulls; clouds, and pretends he doesn't know what a cloud is, and that one there, that's Papa, standing (he checks) on the beach talking to Mr McLennan. Although Papa can't be on the beach *and* in the sky. He feels the sand between his fingers and wonders what this is, too. He smells the wrack on the slats and thinks this is vinegar, Mama's vinegar, for pickling octopus, and the sound of old Haigh singing the worms crawl in and the worms crawl out, and Mama, he can hear her reading about the apostle Jude (October

28), and knows this day has happened before and will again, over and over, unless Papa can get the money from Mr McLennan. But that seems unlikely (he checks, and now they're arguing, and Papa pushes the older man and he steadies himself, and it continues). He notices the midges, as usual, raises his hand and takes some and crushes them and wonders if they're dead, if their mamas and papas will be sad and anyway, some land on his lips and he spits them out, and Terry comes running along the beach and says what are you doing? The boy sits up and says, 'I'm no one.' Terry says what are you talking about, and the boy says I can't be sure who I am or where I'm from and ... what's my name? Terry shakes his head. But sits, and watches their father, up to his ankles in the shallows, argue with Mr McLennan.

The boy says I have no idea how I got here, and his brother says, 'You're not right in the head.' No, the boy says, I'm as right as anything, as Chopin the Polish composer, or Dickens the writer, or some boy in Australia who has to make springs and somehow, something goes wrong, Terry. Do you know what it is? But Terry repeats: 'What went wrong with you?' The boy says nothing, nothing went wrong, and Terry says you shouldn't say these things because Papa has enough problems and shouldn't have to worry about the nonsense coming from your mouth, but the boy says it isn't nonsense, it's what I think, I think he's running, running, and has to get back before the race closes, and if he doesn't someone will lose money, and that will be his fault, all his fault. Terry says, 'Can't you see?' Points to Papa – still shouting at McLennan, and now Mama joins the two men and it settles – and says, 'You read too many books.' The boy says no, not enough, he doesn't read enough books, nine in a house is not enough to know what the world's like. Terry shakes his head again, looks out to sea. 'There's no way we're going anywhere now.' The boy asks why not. Terry says McLennan won't give them their money, and without it they won't have enough, even when they sell their cottage. The boy says Papa should make him pay, but Terry says that's *easier said than done* (Papa's words). McLennan knows lots of people – lawyers, politicians, people in Castlebay who make the rules … people in Edinburgh and Glasgow and London, all over the place, how can you fight that, and it isn't fair, but life isn't fair, Sam.

McLennan storms off, Papa walks after him, and Mama looks at them for a moment then returns to the cottage. Terry says, 'We need to find a treasure.' This interests the boy. He knows there are many books about treasure, and people called *pirates*, and he's seen one but he can only read a few words, so Mama's said patience, listen to Mr Hardy and learn your lessons and one day you'll be able to understand it. That's something to look forward to. Terry says, 'We could do it, you and me.' The boy says what, what could we do, and Terry turns to him and says there used to be smugglers along here. The boy has heard these stories. When a man wanted to bring in a bottle of (say) whisky from France, he'd have to pay the customs man (in Castlebay) a few shillings, pounds, or pence. Why, he isn't sure. But that's what happened. So some men didn't come via Castlebay (or wherever). They landed their boats on the beach, got out with boxes of whisky, buried them, went home and ate kippers. And so when Terry says, 'Just here … they buried a stash here,' and points to the dune behind them, the boy says how do you know? Terry says I was told by someone who knew someone who knew, and they left it here, but they were taken to prison and died and never returned, so now it's here. The boy waits for his brother to grin, but he doesn't, so this is a sign he's telling the truth. He says, 'Why wouldn't someone have dug it up and drunk it all, or sold it all?' Terry smiles and says, 'Only I know.' The boy says how, how do you know, and Terry says he can't say, but it's here, believe me, barrels and barrels of the stuff, and if we dig it up and sell it we can make enough money to go to Australia.

The boy looks out to sea. 'I'm not sure I want to go to Australia, anyway.' Terry says suit yerself then, we can stay here ... as they notice Papa catch up to McLennan and shout at him and it all starts again. The boy suspects this is all a game. But that's not necessarily a bad thing. Maybe clouds are a game? After all, clouds can't be people. The dip's a game, and hopscotch and pull-Sharon's-hair, and songs are a game, and everything's a game. So he says, 'Where did you say?' Terry points to the soft sand, and the boy starts digging with his hands, says this'll take too long, runs back to the shed, finds a shovel, returns, starts the job properly. Meanwhile, Terry says, 'It was Tom Blackbeard, and he had a missing hand where someone chopped it off while he slept, and he made his men dig deep, deep and hide it ...' Now, the boy has an opening, and enlarges this, and says to his brother, 'You help,' but Terry says no, he has to keep a look-out, so the boy continues by himself, and soon he has a tunnel, and it's cold and dark and he shouts back to his brother I can't see anything, are you sure it's here, and Terry says deeper, go on, so they boy uses his hands to continue, throwing out the sand, calling back, 'I can't see anything.' Terry says you need to keep going, you're nearly there, so the boy keeps digging, throwing out sand, and a few minutes later he's so far in he can't see the sun anymore, and he calls to his brother but his brother can't hear and Terry looks around and sees his Mama running towards them calling something, he can't tell, then when he looks back the tunnel is gone – the hole, the very idea of it, and Mama is running and shouting and his Papa sees, too, and comes running, and

Lightning Source UK Ltd.
Milton Keynes UK
UKHW040803111122
412026UK00001B/182